QUEEN HILDEGARDE
BY LAURA E. RICHARDS

CHAPTER I.

HILDEGARDIS GRAHAM.

"And have you decided what is to become of Hilda?" asked Mrs. Graham.

"Hilda?" replied her husband, in a tone of surprise, "Hilda? why, she will go with us, of course. What else should become of the child? She will enjoy the trip immensely, I have no doubt."

Mrs. Graham sighed and shook her head. "I fear that is impossible, dear George!" she said. "To tell the truth, I am a little anxious about Hilda; she is not at all well. I don't mean that she is actually ill," she added quickly, as Mr. Graham looked up in alarm, "but she seems languid and dispirited, has no appetite, and is inclined to be fretful,—an unusual thing for her."

"Needs a change!" said Mr. Graham, shortly. "Best thing for her. Been studying too hard, I suppose, and eating caramels. If I could discover the man who invented that pernicious sweetmeat, I would have him hanged!—hanged, madam!"

"Oh, no, you wouldn't, dear!" said his wife, laughing softly; "I think his life would be quite safe. But about Hilda now! She does need a change, certainly; but is the overland journey in July just the right kind of change for her, do you think?"

Mr. Graham frowned, ran his fingers through his hair, drummed on the table, and then considered his boots attentively. "Well—no!" he said at last, reluctantly. "I—suppose—not. But what can we do with her? Send her to Fred and Mary at the seashore?"

"To sleep in a room seven by twelve, and be devoured by mosquitoes, and have to wear 'good clothes' all the time?" returned Mrs. Graham. "Certainly not."

"Aunt Emily is going to the mountains," suggested Mr. Graham, doubtfully.

"Yes," replied his wife, "with sixteen trunks, a maid, a footman, and three lapdogs! That would never do for Hilda."

"You surely are not thinking of leaving her alone here with the servants?"

The lady shook her head. "No, dear; such poor wits as Heaven granted me are not yet entirely gone, thank you!"

Mr. Graham rose from his chair and flung out both arms in a manner peculiar to him when excited. "Now, now, now, Mildred!" he said impressively, "I have always said that you were a good woman, and I shall continue to assert the same; but you have powers of tormenting that could not be surpassed by the most heartless of your sex. It is perfectly clear, even to my darkened mind, that you have some plan for Hilda fully matured and arranged in that scheming little head of yours; so what is your object in keeping me longer in suspense? Out with it, now! What are you—for of course I am in reality only a cipher (a tolerably large cipher) in the sum—what are you, the commander-in-chief, going to do with Hilda, the lieutenant-general? If you will kindly inform the orderly-sergeant, he will act accordingly, and endeavor to do his duty."

Pretty Mrs. Graham laughed again, and looked up at the six-feet-two of sturdy manhood standing on the hearth-rug, gazing at her with eyes which twinkled merrily under the fiercely frowning brows. "You are a very disorderly-sergeant, dear!" she said. "Just look at your hair! It looks as if all the four winds had been blowing through it—"

"Instead of all the ten fingers going through it," interrupted her husband. "Never mind my hair; that is not the point. What—do—you—propose—to—do—with—your daughter—Hildegarde, or Hildegardis, as it should properly be written?"

"Well, dear George," said the commander-in-chief (she was a very small woman and a very pretty one, though she had a daughter "older than herself," as her husband said; and she wore a soft lilac gown, and had soft, wavy brown hair, and was altogether very pleasant to look at)—"well, dear George, the truth is, I have a little plan, which I should like very much to carry out, if you fully approve of it."

"Ha!" said Mr. Graham, tossing his "tempestuous locks" again, "ho! I thought as much. If I approve, eh, little madam? Better say, whether I approve or not."

So saying, the good-natured giant sat himself down again, and listened while his wife unfolded her plan; and what the plan was, we shall see by and by. Meanwhile let us take a peep at Hilda, or Hildegardis, as she sits in her own room, all unconscious of the plot which is hatching in the parlor below. She is a tall girl of fifteen. Probably she has attained her full height, for she looks as if she had been growing too fast; her form is slender, her face pale, with a weary look in the large gray eyes. It is a delicate, high-bred face, with a pretty nose, slightly "tip-tilted," and a beautiful mouth; but it is half-spoiled by the expression, which is discontented, if not actually peevish. If we lifted the light curling locks of fair hair which lie on her forehead, we should see a very decided frown on a broad white space which ought to be absolutely smooth. Why should a girl of fifteen frown, especially a girl so "exceptionally fortunate" as all her friends considered Hilda Graham? Certainly her surroundings at this moment are pretty enough to satisfy any girl. The room is not large, but it has a sunny bay-window which seems to increase its size twofold. In re-furnishing it a year before, her father had in mind Hilda's favorite flower, the forget-me-not, and the room is simply a bower of forget-me-nots. Scattered over the dull olive ground of the carpet, clustering and nodding from the wall-paper, peeping from the folds of the curtains, the forget-me-nots are everywhere. Even the creamy surface of the toilet-jug and bowl, even the ivory backs of the brushes that lie on the blue-covered toilet table, bear each its cluster of pale-blue blossoms; while the low easy-chair in which the girl is reclining, and the pretty sofa with its plump cushions inviting to repose, repeat the same tale. The tale is again repeated, though in a different way, by a scroll running round the top of the wall, on which in letters of blue and gold is written at intervals: "Ne m'oubliez pas!" "Vergiss mein nicht!" "Non ti scordar!" and the same sentiment is repeated in Spanish, Latin, Greek, and Hebrew, of all which tongues the fond father possessed knowledge.

Is not this indeed a bower, wherein a girl ought to be happy? the bird in the window thinks his blue and gold cage the finest house in the world, and sings as heartily and cheerily as if he had been in the wide green forest; but his mistress does not sing. She sits in the easy-chair, with a book upside-down in her lap, and frowns,—actually frowns, in a forget-me-not bower! There is not much the matter, really. Her head aches, that is all. Her German lesson has been longer and harder than usual, and her father was quite right about the caramels; there is a box of them on the table now, within easy reach of the slim white hand with its forget-me-not ring of blue turquoises. (I do not altogether agree with Mr. Graham about hanging the caramel-maker, but I should heartily like to burn all his wares. Fancy a great mountain of caramels and chocolate-creams and marrons glacés piled up in Union Square, for example, and blazing away merrily,—that is, if the things would burn, which is more than doubtful. How the maidens would weep and wring their hands while the heartless parents chuckled and fed the flames with all the precious treasures of Maillard and Huyler! Ah! it is a pleasant thought, for I who write this am a heartless parent, do you see?)

As I said before, Hilda had no suspicion of the plot which her parents were concocting. She knew that her father was obliged to go to San Francisco, being called suddenly to administer the estate of a cousin who had recently died there, and that her mother and—as she supposed—herself were going with him to offer sympathy and help to the widow, an invalid with three little children. As to the idea of her being left behind; of her father's starting off on a long journey without his lieutenant-general; of her mother's parting from her only child, whom she had watched with tender care and anxiety since the day of her birth,—such a thought never came into Hilda's mind. Wherever her parents went she went, as a matter of course. So it had always been, and so without doubt it always would be. She did not care specially about going to California at this season of the year,—in fact she had told her bosom friend, Madge Everton, only the day before, that it was "rather a bore," and that she should have preferred to go to Newport. "But what would you?" she added, with the slightest shrug of her pretty shoulders. "Papa and mamma really must go, it appears; so of course I must go too."

"A bore!" repeated Madge energetically, replying to the first part of her friend's remarks. "Hilda, what a very singular girl you are! Here I, or Nelly, or any of the other girls would give both our ears, and our front teeth too, to make such a trip; and just because you can go, you sit there and call it 'a bore!'" And Madge shook her black curls, and opened wide eyes of indignation and wonder at our ungrateful heroine. "I only wish," she added, "that you and I could be changed into each other, just for this summer."

"I wish—" began Hilda; but she checked herself in her response to the wish, as the thought of Madge's five brothers rose in her mind (Hilda could not endure boys!), looked attentively at the toe of her little bronze slipper for a few moments, and then changed the subject by proposing a walk. "Console yourself with the caramels, my fiery Madge," she said, pushing the box across the table, "while I put on my boots. We will go to Maillard's and get some more while we are out. His caramels are decidedly better than Huyler's; don't you think so!"

A very busy woman was pretty Mrs. Graham during the next two weeks. First she made an expedition into the country "to see an old friend," she said, and was gone two whole days. And after that she was out every morning, driving hither and thither, from shop to dressmaker, from dressmaker to milliner, from milliner to shoemaker.

3

"It is a sad thing," Mr. Graham would say, when his wife fluttered in to lunch, breathless and exhausted and half an hour late (she, the most punctual of women!),—"it is a sad thing to have married a comet by mistake, thinking it was a woman. How did you find the other planets this morning, my dear? Is it true that Saturn has lost one of his rings? and has the Sun recovered from his last attack of spots? I really fear," he would add, turning to Hilda, "that this preternatural activity in your comet-parent portends some alarming change in the—a—atmospheric phenomena, my child. I would have you on your guard!" and then he would look at her and sigh, shake his head, and apply himself to the cold chicken with melancholy vigor.

Hilda thought nothing of her father's remarks,—papa was always talking nonsense, and she thought she always understood him perfectly. It did occur to her, however, to wonder at her mother's leaving her out on all her shopping expeditions. Hilda rather prided herself on her skill in matching shades and selecting fabrics, and mamma was generally glad of her assistance in all such matters. However, perhaps it was only under-clothing and house-linen, and such things that she was buying. All that was the prosy part of shopping. It was the poetry of it that Hilda loved,—the shimmer of silk and satin, the rich shadows in velvet, the cool, airy fluttering of lawn and muslin and lace. So the girl went on her usual way, finding life a little dull, a little tiresome, and most people rather stupid, but everything on the whole much as usual, if her head only would not ache so; and it was without a shadow of suspicion that she obeyed one morning her mother's summons to come and see her in her dressing-room.

Mr. Graham always spoke of his wife's dressing-room as "the citadel." It was absolutely impregnable, he said. In the open field of the drawing-room or the broken country of the dining-room it might be possible—he had never known such a thing to occur, but still it might be possible—for the commander-in-chief to sustain a defeat; but once intrenched behind the walls of the citadel, horse, foot, and dragoons might storm and charge upon her, but they could not gain an inch. Not an inch, sir! True it was that Mrs. Graham always felt strongest in this particular room. She laughed about it, but acknowledged the fact. Here, on the wall, hung a certain picture which was always an inspiration to her. Here, on the shelf above her desk, were the books of her heart, the few tried friends to whom she turned for help and counsel when things puzzled her. (Mrs. Graham was never disheartened. She didn't believe there was such a word. She was only "puzzled" sometimes, until she saw her way and her duty clear before her, and then she went straight forward, over a mountain or through a stone wall, as the case might be.) Here, in the drawer of her little work-table, were some relics,—a tiny, half-worn shoe, a little doll, a sweet baby face laughing from an ivory frame: the insignia of her rank in the great order of sorrowing mothers; and these, perhaps, gave her that great sympathy and tenderness for all who were in trouble which drew all sad hearts towards her.

And so, on this occasion, the little woman had sat for a few moments looking at the pictured face on the wall, with its mingled majesty and sweetness; had peeped into the best-beloved of all books, and said a little prayer, as was her wont when "puzzled," before she sent the message to Hilda,—for she knew that she must sorely hurt and grieve the child who was half the world to her; and though she did not flinch from the task, she longed for strength and wisdom to do it in the kindest and wisest way.

4

"Hilda, dear," she said gently, when they were seated together on the sofa, hand in hand, with each an arm round the other's waist, as they loved best to sit,—"Hilda, dear, I have something to say that will not please you; something that may even grieve you very much at first." She paused, and Hilda rapidly reviewed in her mind all the possibilities that she could think of. Had anything happened to the box of French dresses which was on its way from Paris? Had a careless servant broken the glass of her fernery again? Had Aunt Emily been saying disagreeable things about her, as she was apt to do? She was about to speak, but at that moment, like a thunderbolt, the next words struck her ear: "We have decided not to take you with us to California." Amazed, wounded, indignant, Hilda could only lift her great gray eyes to meet the soft violet ones which, full of unshed tears, were fixed tenderly upon her. Mrs. Graham continued: "Your father and I both feel, my darling, that this long, fatiguing journey, in the full heat of summer, would be the worst possible thing for you. You have not been very well lately, and it is most important that you should lead a quiet, regular, healthy life for the next few months. We have therefore made arrangements to leave you—"

But here Hilda could control herself no longer. "Mamma! mamma!" she cried. "How can you be so unkind, so cruel? Leave me—you and papa both? Why, I shall die! Of course I shall die, all alone in this great house. I thought you loved me!" and she burst into tears, half of anger, half of grief, and sobbed bitterly.

"Dear child!" said Mrs. Graham, smoothing the fair hair lovingly, "if you had heard me out, you would have seen that we had no idea of leaving you alone, or of leaving you in this house either. You are to stay with—"

"Not with Aunt Emily!" cried the girl, springing to her feet with flashing eyes. "Mamma, I would rather beg in the streets than stay with Aunt Emily. She is a detestable, ill-natured, selfish woman."

"Hildegarde," said Mrs. Graham gravely, "be silent!" There was a moment of absolute stillness, broken only by the ticking of the little crystal clock on the mantelpiece, and then Mrs. Graham continued: "I must ask you not to speak again, my daughter, until I have finished what I have to say; and even then, I trust you will keep silence until you are able to command yourself. You are to stay with my old nurse, Mrs. Hartley, at her farm near Glenfield. She is a very kind, good woman, and will take the best possible care of you. I went to the farm myself last week, and found it a lovely place, with every comfort, though no luxuries, save the great one of a free, healthy, natural life. There, my Hilda, we shall leave you, sadly indeed, and yet feeling that you are in good and loving hands. And I feel very sure," she added in a lighter tone, "that by the time we return, you will be a rosy-cheeked country lass, strong and hearty, with no more thought of headaches, and no wrinkle in your forehead." As she ceased speaking, Mrs. Graham drew the girl close to her, and kissed the white brow tenderly, murmuring: "God bless my darling daughter! If she knew how her mother's heart aches at parting with her!" But Hilda did not know. She was too angry, too bewildered, too deeply hurt, to think of any one except herself. She felt that she could not trust herself to speak, and it was in silence, and without returning her mother's caress, that she rose and sought her own room.

Mrs. Graham looked after her wistfully, tenderly, but made no effort to call her back. The tears trembled in her soft blue eyes, and her lip quivered as she turned to her work-table; but she said quietly to herself: "Solitude is a good medicine. The child will do well, and I know that I have chosen wisely for her."

Bitter tears did Hildegarde shed as she flung herself face downward on her own blue sofa. Angry thoughts surged through her brain. Now she burned with resentment at the parents who could desert her,—their only child; now she melted into pity for herself, and wept more and more as she pictured the misery that lay before her. To be left alone— alone!—on a squalid, wretched farm, with a dirty old woman, a woman who had been a servant,—she, Hildegardis Graham, the idol of her parents, the queen of her "set" among the young people, the proudest and most exclusive girl in New York, as she had once (and not with displeasure) heard herself called!

What would Madge Everton, what would all the girls say! How they would laugh, to hear of Hilda Graham living on a farm among pigs and hens and dirty people! Oh! it was intolerable; and she sprang up and paced the floor, with burning cheeks and flashing eyes.

The thought of opposing the plan did not occur to her. Mrs. Graham's rule, gentle though it was, was not of the flabby, nor yet of the elastic sort. Her decisions were not hastily arrived at; but once made, they were final and abiding. "You might just as well try to oppose the Gulf Stream!" Mr. Graham would say. "They do it sometimes with icebergs, and what is the result? In a few days the great clumsy things are bowing and scraping and turning somersaults, and fairly jostling each other in their eagerness to obey the guidance of the insidious current. Insidious Current, will you allow a cup of coffee to drift in my direction? I shall be only too happy to turn a somersault if it will afford you— thanks!—the smallest gratification."

So Hildegarde's first lessons had been in obedience and in truthfulness; and these were fairly well learned before she began her ABC. And so she knew now, that she might storm and weep as she would in her own room, but that the decree was fixed, and that unless the skies fell, her summer would be passed at Hartley's Glen.

CHAPTER II.

DAME AND FARMER.

When the first shock was over, Hilda was rather glad than otherwise to learn that there was to be no delay in carrying out the odious plan. "The sooner the better," she said to herself. "I certainly don't want to see any of the girls again, and the first plunge will be the worst of it."

"What clothes am I to take?" she asked her mother, in a tone which she mentally denominated "quiet and cold," though possibly some people might have called it "sullen."

"Your clothes are already packed, dear," replied Mrs. Graham; "you have only to pack your dressing-bag, to be all ready for the start to-morrow. See, here is your trunk, locked and strapped, and waiting for the porter's shoulder;" and she showed Hilda a stout, substantial-looking trunk, bearing the initials H.G.

"But, mamma," Hilda began, wondering greatly, "my dresses are all hanging in my wardrobe."

"Not all of them, dear!" said her mother, smiling. "Hark! papa is calling you. Make haste and go down, for dinner is ready."

Wondering more and more, Hildegarde made a hasty toilet, putting on the pretty pale blue cashmere dress which her father specially liked, with silk stockings to match, and dainty slippers of bronze kid. As she clasped the necklace of delicate blue and silver Venetian beads which completed the costume, she glanced into the long cheval-glass which stood between the windows, and could not help giving a little approving nod to her reflection. Though not a great beauty, Hildegarde was certainly a remarkably pretty and even distinguished-looking girl; and "being neither blind nor a fool," she soliloquized, "where is the harm in acknowledging it?" But the next moment the thought came: "What difference will it make, in a stupid farm-house, whether I am pretty or not? I might as well be a Hottentot!" and with the "quiet and cold" look darkening over her face, she went slowly down stairs.

Her father met her with a kiss and clasp of the hand even warmer than usual.

"Well, General!" he said, in a voice which insisted upon being cheery, "marching orders, eh? Marching orders! Break up camp! boot, saddle, to horse and away! Forces to march in different directions, by order of the commander-in-chief." But the next moment he added, in an altered tone: "My girl, mamma knows best; remember that! She is right in this move, as she generally is. Cheer up, darling, and let us make the last evening a happy one!"

Hilda tried to smile, for who could be angry with papa? She made a little effort, and the father and mother made a great one,—how great she could not know; and so the evening passed, better than might have been expected.

The evening passed, and the night, and the next day came; and it was like waking from a strange dream when Hilda found herself in a railway train, with her father sitting beside her, and her mother's farewell kiss yet warm on her cheek, speeding over the open country, away from home and all that she held most dear. Her dressing-bag, with her umbrella neatly strapped to it, was in the rack overhead, the check for her trunk in her pocket. Could it all be true? She tried to listen while her father told her of the happy days he had spent on his grandfather's farm when he was a boy; but the interest was not real, and she found it hard to fix her mind on what he was saying. What did she care about swinging on gates, or climbing apple-trees, or riding unruly colts! She was not a boy, nor even a tomboy. When he spoke of the delights of walking in the country through woodland and meadow, her thoughts strayed to Fifth Avenue, with its throng of well-dressed people, the glittering equipages rolling by, the stately houses on either side, through whose shining windows one caught glimpses of the splendors within; and to the Park, with its shady alleys and well-kept lawns. Could there be any walking so delightful as that which these afforded? Surely not! Ah! Madge and Helen were probably just starting for their walk now. Did they know of her banishment? would they laugh at the thought of Queen Hildegardis vegetating for three months at a wretched—

"Glenfield!" The brakeman's voice rang clear and sharp through the car. Hilda started, and seized her father's hand convulsively.

"Papa!" she whispered, "O papa! don't leave me here; take me home! I cannot bear it!"

"Come, my child!" said Mr. Graham, speaking low, and with an odd catch in his voice; "that is not the way to go into action. Remember, this is your first battle. So, eyes front! charge bayonets! quick step! forward, march!"

The train had stopped. They were on the platform. Mr. Graham led Hilda up to a stout, motherly-looking woman, who held out her hand with a beaming smile.

"Here is my daughter, Mrs. Hartley!" he said, hastily. "You will take good care of her, I know. My darling, good-by! I go on to Dashford, and home by return train in an hour. God bless you, my Hilda! Courage! Up, Guards, and at them! Remember Waterloo!" and he was gone. The engine shrieked an unearthly "Good-by!" and the train rumbled away, leaving Hilda gazing after it through a mist which only her strong will prevented from dissolving in tears.

"Well, my dear," said Dame Hartley's cheery voice, "your papa's gone, and you must not stand here and fret after him. Here is old Nancy shaking her head, and wondering why she does not get home to her dinner. Do you get into the cart, and I will get the station-master to put your trunk in for us."

Hilda obeyed in silence; and climbing into the neat wagon, took her seat and looked about her while Dame Hartley bustled off in search of the station-master. There was not very much to look at at Glenfield station. The low wooden building with its long platform stood on a bare spot of ground, from which the trees all stood back, as if to mark their disapproval of the railway and all that belonged to it. The sandy soil made little attempt to produce vegetation, but put out little humps of rock occasionally, to show what it could do. Behind, a road led off into the woods, hiding itself behind the low-hanging branches of chestnut and maple, ash and linden trees. That was all. Now that the train was gone, the silence was unbroken save by the impatient movements of the old white mare as she shook the flies off and rattled the jingling harness.

Hilda was too weary to think. She had slept little the night before, and the suddenness of the recent changes confused her mind and made her feel as if she were some one else, and not herself at all. She sat patiently, counting half-unconsciously each quiver of Nancy's ears. But now Dame Hartley came bustling back with the station-master, and between the two, Hilda's trunk was hoisted into the cart. Then the good woman climbed in over the wheel, settled her ample person on the seat and gathered up the reins, while the station-master stood smoothing the mare's mane, ready for a parting word of friendly gossip.

"Jacob pooty smart!" he asked, brushing a fly from Nancy's shoulder.

8

"Only middling," was the reply. "He had a touch o' rheumatiz, that last spell of wet weather, and it seems to hang on, kind of. Ketches him in the joints and the small of his back if he rises up suddin."

"I know! I know!" replied the station-master, with eager interest. "Jest like my spells ketches me; on'y I have it powerful bad acrost my shoulders, too. I been kerryin' a potato in my pocket f'r over and above a week now, and I'm in hopes 't'll cure me."

"A potato in your pocket!" exclaimed Dame Hartley. "Reuel Slocum! what do you mean?"

"Sounds curus, don't it?" returned Mr. Slocum. "But it's a fact that it's a great cure for rheumatiz. A grea-at cure! Why, there's Barzillay Smith, over to Peat's Corner, has kerried a potato in his pocket for five years,—not the same potato, y' know; changes 'em when they begin to sprout,—and he hesn't hed a touch o' rheumatism all that time. Not a touch! tol' me so himself."

"Had he ever hed it before?" asked Dame Hartley.

"I d'no as he hed," said Mr. Slocum, "But his father hed; an' his granf'ther before him. So ye see—"

But here Hilda uttered a long sigh of weariness and impatience; and Dame Hartley, with a penitent glance at her, bade good-morning to the victim of rheumatism, gave old Nancy a smart slap with the reins, and drove off down the wood-road.

"My dear child," she said to Hilda as they jogged along, "I ought not to have kept you waiting so long, and you tired with your ride in the cars. But Reuel Slocum lives all alone here, and he does enjoy a little chat with an old neighbor more than most folks; so I hope you'll excuse me."

"It is of no consequence, thank you," murmured Hildegarde, with cold civility. She did not like to be called "my dear child," to begin with; and besides, she was very weary and heartsick, and altogether miserable. But she tried to listen, as the good woman continued to talk in a cheery, comfortable tone, telling her how fond she had always been of "Miss Mildred," as she called Mrs. Graham, and how she had the care of her till she was almost a woman grown, and never would have left her then if Jacob Hartley hadn't got out of patience.

"And to think how you've grown, Hilda dear! You don't remember it, of course, but this isn't the first time you have been at Hartley's Glen. A sweet baby you were, just toddling about on the prettiest little feet I ever saw, when your mamma brought you out here to spend a month with old Nurse Lucy. And your father came out every week, whenever he could get away from his business. What a fine man he is, to be sure! And he and my husband had rare times, shooting over the meadows, and fishing, and the like."

They were still in the wood-road, now jolting along over ridges and hummocks, now ploughing through stretches of soft, sandy soil. Above and on either side, the great trees interlaced their branches, sometimes letting them droop till they brushed against Hilda's cheek, sometimes lifting them to give her a glimpse of cool vistas of dusky green, shade within shade,—moss-grown hollows, where the St. John's-wort showed its tarnished gold, and white Indian pipe gleamed like silver along the ground; or stony beds over which, in the time of the spring rains, little brown brooks ran foaming and bubbling down through the woods. The air was filled with the faint cool smell of ferns, and on every side were great masses of them,—clumps of splendid ostrich-ferns, waving their green plumes in stately pride; miniature forests of the graceful brake, beneath whose feathery branches the wood-mouse and other tiny forest-creatures roamed secure; and in the very road-way, trampled under old Nancy's feet, delicate lady-fern, and sturdy hart's-tongue, and a dozen other varieties, all perfect in grace and sylvan beauty. Hilda was conscious of a vague delight, through all her fatigue and distress How beautiful it was; how cool and green and restful! If she must stay in the country, why could it not be always in the woods, where there was no noise, nor dust, nor confusion?

Her revery was broken in upon by Dame Hartley's voice crying cheerily,—

"And here we are, out of the woods at last! Cheer up, my pretty, and let me show you the first sight of the farm. It's a pleasant, heartsome place, to my thinking."

The trees opened left and right, stepping back and courtesying, like true gentlefolks as they are, with delicate leaf-draperies drooping low. The sun shone bright and hot on a bit of hard, glaring yellow road, and touched more quietly the roofs and chimneys of an old yellow farm-house standing at some distance from the road, with green rolling meadows on every side, and a great clump of trees mounting guard behind it. A low stone wall, with wild-roses nodding over it, ran along the roadside for some way, and midway in it was a trim, yellow-painted gate, which stood invitingly open, showing a neat drive-way, shaded on either side by graceful drooping elms. Old Nancy pricked up her ears and quickened her pace into a very respectable trot, as if she already smelt her oats. Dame Hartley shook her own comfortable shoulders and gave a little sigh of relief, for she too was tired, and glad to get home. But Hilda tightened her grasp on the handle of her dressing-bag, and closed her eyes with a slight shiver of dislike and dread. She would not look at this place. It was the hateful prison where she was to be shut up for three long, weary, dismal months. The sun might shine on it, the trees might wave, and the wild-roses open their slender pink buds; it would be nothing to her. She hated it, and nothing, nothing, nothing could ever make her feel differently. Ah! the fixed and immovable determination of fifteen,—does later life bring anything like it?

But now the wagon stopped, and Hilda must open her eyes, whether she would or no. In the porch, under the blossoming clematis, stood a tall, broad-shouldered man, dressed in rough homespun, who held out his great brown hand and said in a gruff, hearty voice,—

"Here ye be, eh? Thought ye was never comin'. And this is little miss, is it? Howdy, missy? Glad to see ye! Let me jump ye out over the wheel!"

But Hilda declined to be "jumped out;" and barely touching the proffered hand, sprang lightly to the ground.

"Now, Marm Lucy," said Farmer Hartley, "let's see you give a jump like that. 'Tain't so long, seems to me, sence ye used to be as spry as a hoppergrass."

Dame Hartley laughed, and climbed leisurely down from the cart. "Never mind, Jacob!" she said; "I'm spry enough yet to take care of you, if I can't jump as well as I used."

"This missy's trunk?" continued the farmer. "Let me see! What's missy's name now? Huldy, ain't it! Little Huldy! 'Pears to me that's what they used to call ye when ye was here before."

"My name is Hildegardis Graham!" said Hilda in her most icy manner,—what Madge Everton used to call her Empress-of-Russia-in-the-ice-palace-with-the-mercury-sixty-degrees-below-zero manner.

"Huldy Gardies!" repeated Farmer Hartley. "Well, that's a comical name now! Sounds like Hurdy-gurdys, doosn't it? Where did Mis' Graham pick up a name like that, I wonder? But I reckon Huldy'll do for me, 'thout the Gardies, whatever they be."

"Come, father," said Dame Hartley, "the child's tired now, an' I guess she wants to go upstairs. If you'll take the trunk, we'll follow ye."

The stalwart farmer swung the heavy trunk up on his shoulder as lightly as if it were a small satchel, and led the way into the house and up the steep, narrow staircase.

CHAPTER III.

THE PRISONER OF DESPAIR.

As she followed in angry silence, Hilda had a glimpse through a half-open door of a cosey sitting-room; while another door, standing fully open at the other end of the little hall, showed, by a blaze of scarlet tiger-lilies and yellow marigolds, where the garden lay. And now the farmer opened a door and set down the trunk with a heavy thump; and Dame Hartley, taking the girl's hand, led her forward, saying: "Here, my dear, here is your own little room,—the same that your dear mamma slept in when she was here! And I hope you'll be happy in it, Hilda dear, and get all the good we wish for you while you're here!" Hilda bowed slightly, feeling unable to speak; and the good woman continued: "You must be hungry as well as tired, travelling since morning. It's near our dinner-time. Or shall I bring ye up something now,—a cup o' tea and a cooky, eh? Or would you like solid victuals better?"

"Thank you!" said Hilda. "I am not at all hungry; I could not possibly eat anything. My head aches badly!" she added, nervously forestalling her hostess's protestations. "Perhaps a cup of tea later, thank you! I should like to rest now. And I shall not want any dinner."

"Oh! you'll feel better, dear, when you have rested a bit," said Dame Hartley, smoothing the girl's fair hair with a motherly touch, and not seeming to notice her angry shrinking away. "It's the best thing you can do, to lie down and take a good nap; then you'll wake up fresh as a lark, and ready to enjoy yourself. Good-by, dearie! I'll bring up your tea in an hour or so." And with a parting nod and smile, the good woman departed, leaving Hilda, like the heroine of a three-volume novel, "alone with her despair."

Very tragic indeed the maiden looked as she tossed off her hat and flung herself face downward on the bed, refusing to cast even a glance at the cell which was to be her hateful prison. "For of course I shall spend my time here!" she said to herself. "They may send me here, keep me here for years, if they will; but they cannot make me associate with these people." And she recalled with a shudder the gnarled, horny hand which she had touched in jumping from the cart,—she had never felt anything like it; the homely speech, and the nasal twang with which it was delivered; the uncouth garb (good stout butternut homespun!) and unkempt hair and beard of the "odious old savage," as she mentally named Farmer Hartley.

After all, however, Hilda was only fifteen; and after a few minutes, Curiosity began to wake; and after a short struggle with Despair, it conquered, and she sat up on the bed and looked about her.

It was not a very dreadful cell. A bright, clean, fresh little room, all white and blue. White walls, white bedstead, with oh! such snowy coverings, white dimity curtains at the windows, with old-fashioned ball fringes, a little dimity-covered toilet-table, with a quaint looking-glass framed with fat gilt cherubs, all apparently trying to fold their wings in such a way as to enable them to get a peep at themselves in the mirror, and not one succeeding. Then there was a low rocking-chair, and another chair of the high-backed order, and a tall chest of drawers, all painted white, and a wash-hand-stand with a set of dark-blue crockery on it which made the victim of despair open her eyes wide. Hilda had a touch of china mania, and knew a good thing when she saw it; and this deep, eight-sided bowl, this graceful jug with the quaint gilt dragon for a handle, these smaller jugs, boxes, and dishes, all of the same pattern, all with dark-blue dragons (no cold "Canton" blue, but a rich, splendid ultramarine), large and small, prancing and sprawling on a pale buff ground,— what were these things doing in the paltry bedroom of a common farm-house? Hilda felt a new touch of indignation at "these people" for presuming to have such things in their possession.

When her keen eyes had taken in everything, down to the neat rag-carpet on the floor, the girl bethought her of her trunk. She might as well unpack it. Her head could not ache worse, whatever she did; and now that that little imp Curiosity was once awake, he prompted her to wonder what the trunk contained. None of the dresses she had been wearing, she was sure of that; for they were all hanging safely in her wardrobe at home. What surprise had mamma been planning? Well, she would soon know. Hastily unlocking the trunk, she lifted out one tray after another and laid them on the bed. In the first were piles of snowy collars and handkerchiefs, all of plain, fine linen, with no lace or embroidery; a broad-brimmed straw hat with a simple wreath of daisies round it; another hat, a small one, of rough gray felt, with no trimming at all, save a narrow scarlet ribbon; a pair of heavy castor gloves; a couple of white aprons, and one of brown holland, with long sleeves. The next tray was filled with dresses,—dresses which made Hilda's eyes open wide again, as she laid them out, one by one, at full length. There was a dark blue gingham with a red stripe, a brown gingham dotted with yellow daisies, a couple of light

12

calicoes, each with a tiny figure or flower on it, a white lawn, and a sailor-suit of rough blue flannel. All these dresses, and among them all not an atom of trimming. No sign of an overskirt, no ruffle or puff, plaiting or ruching, no "Hamburg" or lace,—nothing! Plain round waists, neatly stitched at throat and wrists; plain round skirts, each with a deep hem, and not so much as a tuck by way of adornment.

Hildegarde drew a deep breath, and looked at the simple frocks with kindling eyes and flushing cheeks. These were the sort of dresses that her mother's servants wore at home. Why was she condemned to wear them now,—she, who delighted in soft laces and dainty embroideries and the clinging draperies which she thought suited her slender, pliant figure so well? Was it a part of this whole scheme; and was the object of the scheme to humiliate her, to take away her self-respect, her proper pride?

Mechanically, but carefully, as was her wont, Hilda hung the despised frocks in the closet, put away the hats, after trying them on and approving of them, in spite of herself ("Of course," she said, "mamma could not get an ugly hat, if she tried!"), and then proceeded to take out and lay in the bureau drawers the dainty under-clothing which filled the lower part of the trunk. Under all was a layer of books, at sight of which Hilda gave a little cry of pleasure. "Ah!" she said, "I shall not be quite alone;" for she saw at a glance that here were some old and dear friends. Lovingly she took them up, one by one: "Romances of the Middle Ages," Percy's "Reliques," "Hereward," and "Westward, Ho!" and, best-beloved of all, the "Adventures of Robin Hood," by grace of Howard Pyle made into so strong an enchantment that the heart thrills even at sight of its good brown cover. And here was her Tennyson and her Longfellow, and Plutarch's Lives, and the "Book of Golden Deeds." Verily a goodly company, such as might even turn a prison into a palace. But what was this, lying in the corner, with her Bible and Prayer-book, this white leather case, with—ah! Hilda—with blue forget-me-nots delicately painted on it? Hastily Hilda took it up and pressed the spring. Her mother's face smiled on her! The clear, sweet eyes looked lovingly into hers; the tender mouth, which had never spoken a harsh or unkind word, seemed almost to quiver as if in life. So kind, so loving, so faithful, so patient, always ready to sympathize, to help, to smile with one's joy or to comfort one's grief,— her own dear, dear mother! A mist came before the girl's eyes. She gazed at the miniature till she could no longer see it; and then, flinging herself down on the pillow again, she burst into a passion of tears, and sobbed and wept as if her heart would break. No longer Queen Hildegardis, no longer the outraged and indignant "prisoner," only Hilda,—Hilda who wanted her mother!

Finally she sobbed herself to sleep,—which was the very best thing she could have done. By and by Dame Hartley peeped softly in, and seeing the child lying "all in a heap," as she said to herself, with her pretty hair all tumbled about, brought a shawl and covered her carefully up, and went quietly away.

"Pretty lamb!" said the good woman. "She'll sleep all the afternoon now, like enough, and wake up feeling a good bit better,—though I fear it will be a long time before your girlie feels at home with Nurse Lucy, Miss Mildred, dear!"

Sure enough, Hilda did sleep all the afternoon; and the soft summer twilight was closing round the farm-house when she woke with a start from a dream of home.

13

"Mamma!" she called quickly, raising herself from the bed. For one moment she stared in amazement at the strange room, with its unfamiliar furnishing; but recollection came only too quickly. She started up as a knock was heard at the door, and Dame Hartley's voice said:

"Hilda, dear, supper is ready, and I am sure you must be very hungry. Will you come down with me?"

"Oh! thank you, presently," said Hildegarde, hastily. "I am not—I haven't changed my dress yet. Don't wait for me, please!"

"Dear heart, don't think of changing your dress!" said Dame Hartley. "You are a country lassie now, you know, and we are plain farm people. Come down just as you are, there's a dear!"

Hilda obeyed, only waiting to wash her burning face and hot, dry hands in the crystal-cold water which she poured out of the blue dragon pitcher. Her hair was brushed back and tied with a ribbon, the little curls combed and patted over her forehead; and in a few minutes she followed her hostess down the narrow staircase, with a tolerably resigned expression on her pretty face. To tell the truth, Hilda felt a great deal better for her long nap; moreover she was a little curious, and very, very hungry,—and oh, how good something did smell!

Mrs. Hartley led the way into the kitchen, as the chief room at Hartley Farm was still called, though the cooking was now done by means of a modern stove in the back kitchen, while the great fireplace, with the crane hanging over it, and the brick oven by its side, was used, as a rule, only to warm the room. At this season the room needed no warming, and feathery asparagus crowned the huge back-log, and nodded between the iron fire-dogs. Ah! it was a pleasant room, the kitchen at Hartley Farm,—wide and roomy, with deep-seated windows facing the south and west; with a floor of dark oak, which shone with more than a century of scrubbing. The fireplace, oven, and cupboards occupied one whole side of the room. Along the other ran a high dresser, whose shelves held a goodly array of polished pewter and brass, shining glass, and curious old china and crockery. Overhead were dark, heavy rafters, relieved by the gleam of yellow "crook-neck" squashes, bunches of golden corn, and long festoons of dried apples. In one window stood the good dame's rocking-chair, with its gay patchwork cushion; and her Bible, spectacles, and work-basket lay on the window-seat beside it. In another was a huge leather arm-chair, which Hilda rightly supposed to be the farmer's, and a wonderful piece of furniture, half desk, half chest of drawers, with twisted legs and cupboards and pigeon-holes and tiny drawers, and I don't know what else. The third window Hilda thought was the prettiest of all. It faced the west, and the full glory of sunset was now pouring through the clustering vines which partly shaded it. The sash was open, and a white rose was leaning in and nodding in a friendly way, as if greeting the new-comer. A low chair and a little work-table, both of quaint and graceful fashion, stood in the recess; and on the window-seat stood some flowering-plants in pretty blue and white pots.

"I suppose I am expected to sit there!" said Hilda to herself. "As if I should sit down in a kitchen!" But all the while she knew in her heart of hearts that this was one of the most attractive rooms she had ever seen, and that that particular corner was pretty enough and picturesque enough for a queen to sit in. You are not to think that she saw all these things at the first glance; far from it. There was something else in the room which claimed the immediate attention of our heroine, and that was a square oak table, shining like a mirror, and covered with good things,—cold chicken, eggs and bacon, golden butter and honey, a great brown loaf on a wonderful carved wooden platter, delicate rolls piled high on a shallow blue dish, and a portly glass jug filled with rich, creamy milk. Here was a pleasant sight for a hungry heroine of fifteen! But alas! at the head of this inviting table sat Farmer Hartley, the "odious savage," in his rough homespun coat, with his hair still very far from smooth (though indeed he had brushed it, and the broad, horny hands were scrupulously clean). With a slight shudder Hilda took the seat which Dame Hartley offered her.

"Well, Huldy," said the farmer, looking up from his eggs and bacon with a cheery smile, "here ye be, eh? Rested after yer journey, be ye?"

"Yes, thank you!" said Hilda, coldly.

"Have some chick'n!" he continued, putting nearly half a chicken on her plate. "An' a leetle bacon, jes' ter liven it up, hey? That's right! It's my idee thet most everythin' 's the better for a bit o' bacon, unless it's soft custard. I d' 'no ez thet 'ud go with it pitickler. Haw! haw!"

Hilda kept her eyes on her plate, determined to pay no attention to the vulgar pleasantries of this unkempt monster. It was hard enough to eat with a steel fork, without being further tormented. But the farmer seemed determined to drag her into conversation.

"How's yer ha-alth in gineral, Huldy? Pooty rugged, be ye? Seems to me ye look kin' o' peaked."

"I am quite well!" It was Queen Hildegarde who spoke now, in icy tones; but her coldness had no effect on her loquacious host.

"I s'pose ye'll want ter lay by a day or two, till ye git used ter things, like; but then I sh'll want ye ter take holt. We're short-handed now, and a smart, likely gal kin be a sight o' help. There's the cows ter milk—the' ain't but one o' them thet's real ugly, and she only kicks with the off hind-leg; so 't's easy enough ter look out for her."

Hilda looked up in horror and amazement, and caught a twinkle in the farmer's eye which told her that he was quizzing her. The angry blood surged up even to the roots of her hair; but she disdained to reply, and continued to crumble her bread in silence.

"Father, what ails you?" said kind Dame Hartley. "Why can't you let the child alone? She's tired yet, and she doesn't understand your joking ways.—Don't you mind the farmer, dear, one bit; his heart's in the right place, but he do love to tease."

But the good woman's gentle words were harder to bear, at that moment, than her husband's untimely jesting. Hilda's heart swelled high. She felt that in another moment the

15

tears must come; and murmuring a word of excuse, she hastily pushed back her chair and left the room.

An hour after, Hilda was sitting by the window of her own room, looking listlessly out on the soft summer evening, and listening to the melancholy cry of the whippoorwill, when she heard voices below. The farmer was sitting with his pipe in the vine-clad porch just under the window; and now his wife had joined him, after "redding up" the kitchen, and giving orders for the next morning to the tidy maidservant.

"Well, Marm Lucy," said Farmer Hartley's gruff, hearty voice, "now thet you have your fine bird, I sh'd like to know what you're a-goin' to do with her. She's as pretty as a pictur, but a stuck-up piece as ever I see. Don't favor her mother, nor father either, as I can see."

"Poor child!" said Dame Hartley, with a sigh, "I fear she will have a hard time of it before she comes to herself. But I promised Miss Mildred that I would try my best; and you said you would help me, Jacob."

"So I did, and so I will!" replied the farmer. "But tell me agin, what was Miss Mildred's idee? I got the giner'l drift of it, but I can't seem to put it together exactly. I didn't s'pose the gal was this kind, anyhow."

"She told me," Dame Hartley said, "that this child—her only one, Jacob! you know what that means—was getting into ways she didn't like. Going about with other city misses, who cared for nothing but pleasure, and who flattered and petted her because of her beauty and her pretty, proud ways (and maybe because of her father's money too; though Miss Mildred didn't say that), she was getting to think too much of herself, and to care too much for fine dresses and sweetmeats and idle chatter about nothing at all." (How Hilda's cheeks burned as she remembered the long séances in her room, she on the sofa, and Madge in the arm-chair, with the box of Huyler's or Maillard's best always between them! Had they ever talked of anything "worth the while," as mamma would say? She remembered mamma's coming in upon them once or twice, with her sweet, grave face. She remembered, too, a certain uneasy feeling she had had for a moment—only for a moment—when the door closed behind her mother. But Madge had laughed, and said, "Isn't your mother perfectly sweet? She doesn't mind a bit, does she?" and she had answered, "Oh, no!" and had forgotten it in the account of Helen McIvor's new bonnet.) "And then Miss Mildred said, 'I had meant to take her into the country with me this summer, and try to show the child what life really means, and let her learn to know her brothers and sisters in the different walks of this life, and how they live, and what they do. I want her to see for herself what a tiny bit of the world, and what a silly, useless, gilded bit, is the little set of fashionable girls whom she has chosen for her friends. But this sudden call to California has disarranged all my plans. I cannot take her with me there, for the child is not well, and country air and quiet are necessary for her bodily health. And so, Nurse Lucy,' she says, 'I want you to take my child, and do by her as you did by me!'

"'Oh! Miss Mildred,' I said, 'do you think she can be happy or contented here? I'll do my best; I'm sure you know that! But if she's as you say, she is a very different child to what you were, Miss Mildred dear.'

16

"'She will not be happy at first,' says Miss Mildred. 'But she has a really noble nature, Nurse Lucy, and I am very sure that it will triumph over the follies and faults which are on the outside.'

"And then she kissed me, the dear! and came up and helped me set the little room to rights, and kissed the pillows, sweet lady, and cried over them a bit. Ah me! 'tis hard parting from our children, even for a little while, that it is."

Dame Hartley paused and sighed. Then she said: "And so, here the child is, for good or for ill, and we must do our very best by her, Jacob, you as well as I. What ailed you to-night, to tease her so at supper? I thought shame of you, my man."

"Well, Marm Lucy," said the farmer, "I don't hardly know what ailed me. But I tell ye what, 'twas either laugh or cry for me, and I thought laughin' was better nor t'other. To see that gal a-settin' there, with her pretty head tossed up, and her fine, mincin' ways, as if 'twas an honor to the vittles to put them in her mouth; and to think of my maid—" He stopped abruptly, and rising from the bench, began to pace up and down the garden-path. His wife joined him after a moment, and the two walked slowly to and fro together, talking in low tones, while the soft summer darkness gathered closer and closer, and the pleasant night-sounds woke, cricket and katydid and the distant whippoorwill filling the air with a cheerful murmur.

Long, long sat Hildegarde at the window, thinking more deeply than she had ever thought in her life before. Different passions held her young mind in control while she sat motionless, gazing into the darkness with wide-open eyes. First anger burned high, flooding her cheek with hot blushes, making her temples throb and her hands clench themselves in a passion of resentment. But to this succeeded a mood of deep sadness, of despair, as she thought; though at fifteen one knows not, happily, the meaning of despair.

Was this all true? Was she no better, no wiser, than the silly girls of her set? She had always felt herself so far above them mentally; they had always so frankly acknowledged her supremacy; she knew she was considered a "very superior girl:" was it true that her only superiority lay in possessing powers which she never chose to exert? And then came the bitter thought: "What have I ever done to prove myself wiser than they?" Alas for the answer! Hilda hid her face in her hands, and it was shame instead of anger that now sent the crimson flush over her cheeks. Her mother despised her! Her mother—perhaps her father too! They loved her, of course; the tender love had never failed, and would never fail. They were proud of her too, in a way. And yet they despised her; they must despise her! How could they help it? Her mother, whose days were a ceaseless round of work for others, without a thought of herself; her father, active, energetic, business-like,—what must her life seem to them? How was it that she had never seen, never dreamed before, that she was an idle, silly, frivolous girl? The revelation came upon her with stunning force. These people too, these coarse country people, despised her and laughed at her! The thought was more than she could bear. She sprang up, feeling as if she were suffocating, and walked up and down the little room with hurried and nervous steps. Then suddenly there came into her mind one sentence of her mother's that Dame Hartley had repeated: "Hilda has a really noble nature—" What was the rest? Something about triumphing over the faults and follies which lay outside. Had her mother really said that? Did she believe, trust in, her silly daughter? The girl stood still, with clasped hands and

17

bowed head. The tumult within her seemed to die away, and in its place something was trembling into life, the like of which Hilda Graham had never known, never thought of, before; faint and timid at first, but destined to gain strength and to grow from that one moment,—a wish, a hope, finally a resolve.

CHAPTER IV.

THE NEW HILDA.

The morning came laughing into Hilda's room, and woke her with such a flash of sunshine and trill of bird-song that she sprang up smiling, whether she would or no. Indeed, she felt happier than she could have believed to be possible. The anger, the despair, even the self-humiliation and anguish of repentance, were gone with the night. Morning was here,—a new day and a new life. "Here is the new Hildegarde!" she cried as she plunged her face into the clear, sparkling water. "Do you see me, blue dragons? Shake paws, you foolish creatures, and don't stand ramping and glaring at each other in that way! Here is a new girl come to see you. The old one was a minx,—do you hear, dragons?" The dragons heard, but were too polite to say anything; and as for not ramping, why they had ramped and glared for fifty years, and had no idea of making a change at their time of life.

The gilt cherubs round the little mirror were more amiable, and smiled cheerfully at Hilda as she brushed and braided her hair, and put on the pretty blue gingham frock. "We have no clothes ourselves," they seemed to say, "but we appreciate good ones when we see them!" Indeed, the frock fitted to perfection. "And after all," said the new Hilda as she twirled round in front of the glass, "what is the use of an overskirt?" after which astounding utterance, this young person proceeded to do something still more singular. After a moment's hesitation she drew out one of the white aprons which she had scornfully laid in the very lowest drawer only twelve hours before, tied it round her slender waist, and then, with an entirely satisfied little nod at the mirror, she tripped lightly downstairs and into the kitchen. Dame Hartley was washing dishes at the farther end of the room, in her neat little cedar dish-tub, with her neat little mop; and she nearly dropped the blue and white platter from her hands when she heard Hilda's cheerful "Good morning, Nurse Lucy!" and, turning, saw the girl smiling like a vision of morning.

"My dear," she cried, "sure I thought you were fast asleep still. I was going up to wake you as soon as I had done my dishes. And did you sleep well your first night at Hartley's Glen?"

"Oh, yes! I slept very sound indeed," said Hilda, lightly. And then, coming close up to Dame Hartley, she said in an altered tone, and with heightened color: "Nurse Lucy, I did not behave well last night, and I want to tell you that I am sorry. I am not like mamma, but I want to grow a little like her, if I can, and you must help me, please!"

Her voice faltered, and good Nurse Lucy, laying down her mop, took the slender figure in her motherly arms, from which it did not now shrink away.

"My lamb!" she said; "Miss Mildred's own dear child! You look liker your blessed mother this minute than I ever thought you would. Help you? That I will, with all my heart!—though I doubt if you need much help, coming to yourself so soon as this. Well, well!"

"Coming to herself!" It was the same phrase the good dame had used the night before, and it struck Hilda's mind with renewed force. Yes, she had come to herself,—her new self, which was to be so different from the old. How strange it all was! What should she do now, to prove the new Hilda and try her strength? Something must be done at once; the time for folded hands and listless revery was gone by.

"Shall I—may I help you to get breakfast?" she asked aloud, rather timidly.

"Breakfast? Bless you, honey, we had breakfast two hours ago. We farmers are early birds, you know. But you can lay a plate and napkin for yourself, if you like, while I drop a couple of fresh eggs and toast a bit of bacon for you. Do you like bacon, then?"

Rather disappointed at the failure of her first attempt to be useful, Hilda laid the snowy napkin on the shining table, and chose a pretty blue and white plate from the well-stocked shelves of the dresser.

"And now open that cupboard, my lamb," said her hostess, "and you'll find the loaf, and a piece of honeycomb, and some raspberries. I'll bring a pat of butter and some milk from the dairy, where it's all cool for you."

"Raspberries!" cried Hilda. "Oh, how delightful! Why, the dew is still on them, Nurse Lucy! And how pretty they look, with the cool green leaves round them!"

"Ay!" said the good woman, "Jacob brought them in not ten minutes ago. He thought you would like them fresh from the bushes."

Hilda's cheek rivalled the raspberries in bloom as she bent over them to inhale their fragrance. The farmer had picked these himself for her,—had probably left his work to do so; and she had called him an odious old savage, and an unkempt monster, and—oh dear! decidedly, the old Hilda was a very disagreeable girl. But here were the eggs, each blushing behind its veil of white, and here was the milk, and a little firm nugget in a green leaf, which was too beautiful to be butter, and yet too good to be anything else. And the new Hilda might eat her breakfast with a thankful heart, and did so. The white rose nodded to her from the west window much more cordially than it had done the night before. It even brought out a little new bud to take a peep at the girl who now smiled, instead of scowling, across the room. The vines rustled and shook, and two bright black eyes peeped between the leaves. "Tweet!" said the robin, ruffling his scarlet waistcoat a little. "When you have quite finished your worms, you may come out, and I will show you the garden. There are cherries!" and away he flew, while Hilda laughed and clapped her hands, for she had understood every word.

"May I go out into the garden?" she asked, when she had finished her breakfast and taken her first lesson in dish-washing, in spite of Dame Hartley's protest. "And isn't there something I can do there, please? I want to work; I don't want to be idle any longer."

"Well, honey," replied the dame, "there are currants to pick, if you like such work as that. I am going to make jelly to-morrow; and if you like to begin the picking, I will come and help you when my bread is out of the oven."

Gladly Hilda flew up to her room for the broad-leaved hat with the daisy-wreath; and then, taking the wide, shallow basket which Dame Hartley handed her, she fairly danced out of the door, over the bit of green, and into the garden.

Ah! the sweet, heartsome country garden that this was,—the very thought of it is a rest and a pleasure. Straight down the middle ran a little gravel path, with a border of fragrant clove-pinks on either side, planted so close together that one saw only the masses of pale pink blossoms resting on their bed of slender silvery leaves. And over the border! Oh the wealth of flowers, the blaze of crimson and purple and gold, the bells that swung, the spires that sprang heavenward, the clusters that nodded and whispered together in the morning breeze! Here were ranks upon ranks of silver lilies, drawn up in military fashion, and marshalled by clumps of splendid tiger-lilies,—the drum-majors of the flower-garden. Here were roses of every sort, blushing and paling, glowing in gold and mantling in crimson. And the carnations showed their delicate fringes, and the geraniums blazed, and the heliotrope languished, and the "Puritan pansies" lifted their sweet faces and looked gravely about, as if reproving the other flowers for their frivolity; while shy Mignonette, thinking herself well hidden behind her green leaves, still made her presence known by the exquisite perfume which all her gay sisters would have been glad to borrow.

Over all went the sunbeams, rollicking and playing; and through all went Hildegarde, her heart filled with a new delight, feeling as if she had never lived before. She talked to the flowers. She bent and kissed the damask rose, which was too beautiful to pluck. She put her cheek against a lily's satin-silver petals, and started when an angry bee flew out and buzzed against her nose. But where were the currant-bushes? Ah! there they were,—a row of stout green bushes, forming a hedge at the bottom of the garden.

Hilda fell busily to work, filling her basket with the fine, ruddy clusters. "How beautiful they are!" she thought, holding up a bunch so that the sunlight shone through it. "And these pale, pinky golden ones, which show all the delicate veins inside. Really, I must eat this fat bunch; they are like fairy grapes! The butler fay comes and picks a cluster every evening, and carries it on a lily-leaf platter to the queen as she sits supping on honey-cakes and dew under the damask rose-bush."

While fingers and fancy were thus busily employed, Hilda was startled by the sound of a voice which seemed to come from beyond the currant-bushes, very near her. She stood quite still and listened.

"A-g, ag," said the voice; "g-l-o-m, glom,—agglom; e-r er,—agglomer; a-t-e, ate,—agglomerate." There was a pause, and then it began again: "A-g, ag; g-l-o-m, glom," etc.

Hilda's curiosity was now thoroughly aroused; and laying down her basket, she cautiously parted the leaves and peeped through. She hardly knew what she expected to see. What she did see was a boy about ten years old, in a flannel shirt and a pair of ragged breeches, busily weeding a row of carrots; for this was the vegetable garden, which lay behind the currant-bushes. On one side of the boy was a huge heap of weeds; on the other lay a tattered book, at which he glanced from time to time, though without leaving his work. "A-n, an," he was now saying; "t-i, ti,—anti; c-i-p, cip,—anticip; a-t-e, ate,—anticipate. 'To expect.' Well! that is a good un. Why can't they say expect, 'stead o' breakin' their jawsen with a word like that? Anticip-ate! Well, I swan! I hope he enjoyed eatin' it. Sh'd think 't'd ha giv' him the dyspepsy, anyhow."

At this Hilda could contain herself no longer, but burst into a merry peal of laughter; and as the boy started up with staring eyes and open mouth, she pushed the bushes aside and came towards him. "I am sorry I laughed," she said, not unkindly. "You said that so funnily, I couldn't help it. You did not pronounce the word quite right, either. It is anticipate, not anticip-ate."

"SHE PUSHED THE BUSHES ASIDE AND CAME TOWARDS HIM"
"SHE PUSHED THE BUSHES ASIDE AND CAME TOWARDS HIM"
The boy looked half bewildered and half grateful. "Anticipate!" he repeated, slowly. "Thanky, miss! it's a onreasonable sort o' word, 'pears ter me." And he bent over his carrots again.

But Hilda did not return to her currant-picking. She was interested in this freckled, tow-headed boy, wrestling with four-syllabled words while he worked.

"Why do you study your lesson out here?" she asked, sitting down on a convenient stump, and refreshing herself with another bunch of white currants. "Couldn't you learn it better indoors?"

"Dunno!" replied the boy. "Ain't got no time ter stay indoors."

"You might learn it in the evening!" suggested Hilda.

"I can't keep awake evenin's," said the boy, simply. "Hev to be up at four o'clock to let the cows out, an' I git sleepy, come night. An' I like it here too," he added. "I can l'arn 'em easier, weedin'; take ten weeds to a word."

"Ten weeds to a word?" repeated Hilda. "I don't understand you."

"Why," said the boy, looking up at her with wide-open blue eyes, "I take a good stiff word (I like 'em stiff, like that an—anticipate feller), and I says it over and over while I pull up ten weeds,—big weeds, o' course, pusley and sich. I don't count chickweed. By the time the weeds is up, I know the word, I've larned fifteen this spell!" and he glanced proudly at his tattered spelling-book as he tugged away at a mammoth root of pusley, which stretched its ugly, sprawling length of fleshy arms on every side.

Hilda watched him for some moments, many new thoughts revolving in her head. How many country boys were there who taught themselves in this way? How many, among the clever girls at Mademoiselle Haut-ton's school, had this sort of ambition to learn, of pride in learning? Had she, the best scholar in her class, had it? She had always known her lessons, because they were easy for her to learn, because she had a quick eye and ear, and a good memory. She could not help learning, Mademoiselle said. But this,—this was something different!

"What is your name?" she asked, with a new interest.

"Bubble Chirk," replied the freckled boy, with one eye on his book, and the other measuring a tall spire of pigweed, towards which he stretched his hand.

"What!" cried Hilda, in amazement.

"Bubble Chirk!" said the boy. "Kin' o' curus name, ain't it? The hull of it's Zerubbabel Chirk; but most folks ain't got time to say all that. It trips you up, too, sort o'. Bubble's what they call me; 'nless it's Bub."

The contrast between the boy's earnest and rather pathetic face, and his absurdly volatile name, was almost too much for Hilda's gravity. But she checked the laugh which rose to her lips, and asked: "Don't you go to school at all, Bubble? It is a pity that you shouldn't, when you are so fond of study."

"Gin'lly go for a spell in the winter," replied Bubble. "They ain't no school in summer, y' know. Boys hes to work, round here. Mam ain't got nobody but me 'n Pink, sence father died."

"Who is Pink?" asked Hilda, gently.

"My sister," replied Bubble. "Thet ain't her real name, nuther. Mam hed her christened Pinkrosia, along o' her bein' so fond o' roses, Mam was; but we don't call her nothin' only Pink."

"Pink Chirk!" repeated Hilda to herself. "What a name! What can a girl be like who is called Pink Chirk?"

But now Bubble seemed to think that it was his turn to ask questions. "I reckon you're the gal that's come to stay at Mr. Hartley's?" he said in an interrogative tone.

Hilda's brow darkened for a moment at the word "gal," which came with innocent frankness from the lips of the ragged urchin before her. But the next moment she remembered that it was only the old Hilda who cared about such trifles; so she answered pleasantly enough:

"Yes, I am staying at Mr. Hartley's. I only came yesterday, but I am to stay some time."

"And what mought your name be?" inquired Master Chirk.

"Hildegardis Graham." It was gently said, in a very different voice from that which had answered Farmer Hartley in the same words the night before; but it made a startling impression on Bubble Chirk.

"Hildy—" he began; and then, giving it up, he said simply: "Well, I swan! Do ye kerry all that round with ye all the time?"

Hilda laughed outright at this.

"Oh, no!" she said; "I am called Hilda generally."

"But you kin spell the hull of it?" asked the boy anxiously.

"Yes, certainly!" Bubble's eager look subsided into one of mingled awe and admiration.

"Reckon ye must know a heap," he said, rather wistfully. "Wish't I did!"

Hilda looked at him for a moment without speaking. Her old self was whispering to her. "Take care what you do!" it said. "This is a coarse, common, dirty boy. He smells of the stable; his hair is full of hay; his hands are beyond description. What have you in common with such a creature? He has not even the sense to know that he is your inferior." "I don't care!" said the new Hilda. "I know what mamma would do if she were here, and I shall do it,—or try to do it, at least. Hold your tongue, you supercilious minx!"

"Bubble," she said aloud, "would you like me to teach you a little, while I am here? I think perhaps I could help you with your lessons."

The boy looked up with a sudden flash in his blue eyes, while his face grew crimson with pleasure.

"Would I like it?" he cried eagerly. But the next moment the glow faded, and he looked awkwardly down at his ragged book and still more ragged clothes. "Guess I ain't no time to l'arn that way," he muttered in confusion.

"Nonsense!" said Hilda, decidedly. "There must be some hour in the day when you can be spared. I shall speak to Farmer Hartley about it. Don't look at your clothes, you foolish boy," she continued, with a touch of Queen Hildegardis' quality, yet with a kindly intonation which was new to that potentate. "I am not going to teach your clothes. You are not your clothes!" cried Her Majesty, wondering at herself, and a little flushed with her recent victory over the "minx." The boy's face brightened again.

"That's so!" he said, joyously; "that's what Pink says. But I didn't s'pose you'd think so," he added, glancing bashfully at the delicate, high-bred face, with its flashing eyes and imperial air.

"I do think so!" said Hilda. "So that is settled, and we will have our first lesson to-morrow. What would you—"

"Hilda! Hilda! where are you, dear?" called Dame Hartley's voice from the other side of the currant-bush-hedge. And catching up her basket, and bidding a hasty good-by to her new acquaintance and future scholar, Hildegarde darted back through the bushes.

Zerubbabel Chirk looked after her a few moments, with kindling eyes and open mouth of wonder and admiration.

"Wall!" he said finally, after a pause of silent meditation, "I swan! I reelly do! I swan to man!" and fell to weeding again as if his life depended on it.

CHAPTER V.

THE BLUE PLATTER.

"Merry it is in the green forést,
Among the leavés green!"
Thus sang Hildegarde as she sat in the west window, busily stringing her currants. She had been thinking a great deal about Bubble Chirk, making plans for his education, and wondering what his sister Pink was like. He reminded her, she could not tell why, of the "lytel boy" who kept fair Alyce's swine, in her favorite ballad of "Adam Bell, Clym o' the Clough, and William of Cloudeslee;" and the words of the ballad rose half unconsciously to her lips as she bent over the great yellow bowl, heaped with scarlet and pale-gold clusters.

"Merry it is in the green forést,
Among the leavés green,
Whenas men hunt east and west
With bows and arrowés keen,

"For to raise the deer out of their denne,—
Such sights have oft been seen;
As by three yemen of the north countree:
By them it is, I mean.

"The one of them hight Adam Bell,
The other Clym o' the Clough;
The third was Willyam of Cloudeslee,—
An archer good enough.

"They were outlawed for venison,
These yemen every one.
They swore them brethren on a day
To English wood for to gone.

"Now lythe and listen, gentylmen,
That of myrthes loveth to hear!"
At this moment the door opened, and Farmer Hartley entered, taking off his battered straw hat as he did so, and wiping his forehead with a red bandanna handkerchief. Hilda looked up with a pleasant smile, meaning to thank him for the raspberries which he had gathered for her breakfast; but to her utter astonishment the moment his eyes fell upon her he gave a violent start and turned very pale; then, muttering something under his breath, he turned hastily and left the room.

24

"Oh! what is the matter?" cried Hilda, jumping up from her chair. "What have I done, Nurse Lucy? I have made the farmer angry, somehow. Is this his chair? I thought—"

"No, no, honey dear!" said Nurse Lucy soothingly. "Sit ye down; sit ye down! You have done nothing. I'm right glad of it," she added, with a tone of sadness in her pleasant voice. "Seeing as 'tis all in God's wisdom, Jacob must come to see it so; and 'tis no help, but a deal of hindrance, when folks set aside chairs and the like, and see only them that's gone sitting in them." Then, seeing Hilda's look of bewilderment, she added, laying her hand gently on the girl's soft hair: "You see, dear, we had a daughter of our own this time last year. Our only one she was, and just about your age,—the light of our eyes, our Faith. She was a good girl, strong and loving and heartsome, and almost as pretty as yourself, Hilda dear; but the Father had need of her, so she was taken from us for a while. It was cruel hard for Jacob; cruel, cruel hard. He can't seem to see, even now, that it was right, or it wouldn't have been so. And so I can tell just what he felt, coming in just now, sudden like, and seeing you sitting in Faith's chair. Like as not he forgot it all for a minute, and thought it was herself. She had a blue dress that he always liked, and she'd sit here and sing, and the sun coming in on her through her own window there, as she always called it: like a pretty picture she was, our Faith."

"Oh!" cried Hilda, taking the brown, motherly hand in both of hers, "I am so very, very sorry, dear Nurse Lucy! I did not know! I will never sit here again. I thought—"

But she was ashamed to say what she had thought,—that this chair and table had been set for her to tempt her to sit down "in a kitchen!" She could hear herself say it as she had said it last night, with a world of scornful emphasis. How long it seemed since last night; how much older she had grown! And yet—and yet somehow she felt a great deal younger.

All this passed through her mind in a moment; but Nurse Lucy was petting her, and saying: "Nay, dearie; nay, child! This is just where I want you to sit. 'Twill be a real help to Farmer, once he is used to it. Hark! I hear him coming now. Sit still! To please me, my dear, sit still where ye are."

"SHE BENT IN REAL DISTRESS OVER THE CURRANTS."
"SHE BENT IN REAL DISTRESS OVER THE CURRANTS."
Hilda obeyed, though her heart beat painfully; and she bent in real distress over the currants as Farmer Hartley once more entered the room. She hardly knew what she feared or expected; but her relief was great when he bade her a quiet but cheerful "Good-day!" and crossing the room, sat down in his great leather arm-chair.

"Dinner'll be ready in five minutes, Jacob!" said the good dame, cheerily; "I've only to lay the table and dish the mutton."

"Oh! let me help," cried Hilda, springing up and setting her bowl of currants on the window-sill.

So between the two the snowy cloth was laid, and the blue plates and the shining knives and forks laid out. Then they all sat down, and the little maid-servant came too,

25

and took her place at the end of the table; and presently in came a great loutish-looking fellow, about one or two and twenty, with a great shock of sandy hair and little ferret-eyes set too near together, whom Dame Hartley introduced as her nephew. He sat down too, and ate more than all the rest of them put together. At sight of this man, who gobbled his food noisily, and uttered loud snorts between the mouthfuls, the old Hilda awoke in full force. She could not endure this; mamma never could have intended it! The Hartleys were different, of course. She was willing to acknowledge that she had been in the wrong about them; but this lout, this oaf, this villainous-looking churl,—to expect a lady to sit at the same table with him: it was too much! She would ask if she might not dine in her own room after this, as apparently it was only at dinner that this "creature" made his appearance.

Farmer Hartley had been very silent since he came in, but now he seemed to feel that he must make an effort to be sociable, so he said kindly, though gravely,—

"I see ye're lookin' at that old dish, Huldy. 'Tis a curus old piece, 'n' that's a fact. Kin ye read the motter on it?"

Hilda had not been looking at the dish, though her eyes had been unconsciously fixed upon it, and she now bent forward to examine it. It was an oblong platter, of old blue and white crockery. In the middle (which was now visible, as the "creature" had just transferred the last potato to his own plate, stabbing it with his knife for that purpose) was a quaint representation of a mournful-looking couple, clad in singularly ill-fitting aprons of fig-leaves. The man was digging with a spade, while the woman sat at a spinning-wheel placed dangerously near the edge of the deep ditch which her husband had already dug. Round the edge ran an inscription, which, after some study, Hilda made out to be the old distich:

"When Adam delved, and Eve span,
Where was then the gentleman?"
Hilda burst out laughing in spite of her self.

"Oh, it is wonderful!" she cried. "Who ever heard of Eve with a spinning-wheel? Where did this come from, Farmer Hartley? I am sure it must have a history."

"Wa-al," said the farmer, smiling, "I d'no ez 't' hes so to speak a hist'ry, an' yit there's allays somethin' amoosin' to me about that platter. My father was a sea-farin' man most o' his life, an' only came to the farm late in life, 'count of his older brother dyin', as owned it. Well, he'd picked up a sight o' queer things in his voyages, father had; he kep' some of 'em stowed away in boxes, and brought 'em out from time to time, ez he happened to think of 'em. Wa-al, we young uns growed up (four of us there was, all boys, and likely boys too, if I do say it), and my brother Simon, who was nex' to me, he went to college. He was a clever chap, Simon was, an' nothin' would do for him but he must be a gentleman.

"'Jacob kin stick to the farm an' the mill; if he likes,' says he, 'an' Tom kin go to sea, an' William kin be a minister,—'t's all he's good fer, I reckon; but I'm goin' ter be a gentleman!' says Simon. He said it in father's hearin' one day, an' father lay back in his cheer an' laughed; he was allays laughin', father was. An' then he went off upstairs, an' we heard him rummagin' about among his boxes up in the loft-chamber. We dassn't none of us tech them boxes, we boys, though we warn't afeard of nothin' else in the world, only father. Presently he comes down again, still a-laughin', an' kerryin' that platter in his hand. He sets it down afore Simon, an' says he, 'Wealthy,' says he (that was my mother), 'Wealthy,' says he, 'let Simon have his victuals off o' this platter every day, d'ye hear? The' ain't none other that's good enough for him!' an' then he laughed again, till he fairly shook, an' Simon looked black as thunder, an' took his hat an' went out. An' so after Simon went to college, every time he come home for vacation and set down to table with his nose kind o' turned up, like he was too good to set with his own kith and kin, father 'ud go an git the old blue platter and set it afore him, an' say, 'Here's your dish, Simon; been diggin' any lately, my son?' and then lay back in his cheer and laugh."

"And did Simon become—a—a gentleman?" asked Hilda, taking her own little lesson very meekly, in her desire to know more.

Farmer Hartley's brow clouded instantly, and the smile vanished from his lips. "Poor Simon!" he said, sadly. "He might ha' been anythin' he liked, if he'd lived and—been fortunate."

"Simon Hartley is dead, Hilda dear," interposed Dame Hartley, gently; "he died some years ago. Will you have some of your own currants, my dear?—Hilda has been helping me a great deal, Father," she added, addressing her husband. "I don't know how I should have got all my currants picked without her help."

"Has she so?" exclaimed the farmer, fixing his keen gray eyes on the girl. "Waal! waal! to think o' that! Why, we sh'll hev her milkin' that cow soon, after all; hey, Huldy?"

Hildegarde looked up bravely, with a little smile. "I will try," she said, cheerfully, "if you will risk the milk, Farmer Hartley."

The old farmer returned her smile with one so bright and kind and genial that somehow the ice bent, then cracked, and then broke. The old Hilda shrank into so small a space that there was really very little left of her, and the new Hilda rose from table feeling that she had gained a new friend.

So it came to pass that about an hour later our heroine was walking beside the farmer on the way to the barnyard, talking merrily, and swinging the basket which she was going to fill with eggs. "But how shall I find them," she asked, "if the hens hide them away so carefully?"

"Oh, you'll hear 'em scrattlin' round!" replied the farmer. "They're gret fools, hens are,—greter than folks, as a rule; an' that is sayin' a good deal."

They crossed the great sunny barn-yard, and paused at the barn-door, while Hilda looked in with delight. A broad floor, big enough for a ballroom, with towering walls of fragrant hay on either side reaching up to the rafters; great doors open at the farther end, showing a snatch of blue, radiant sky, and a lovely wood-road winding away into deep thickets of birch and linden; dusty, golden, cobwebby sunbeams slanting down through the little windows, and touching the tossed hay-piles into gold; and in the middle, hanging by iron chains from the great central beam, a swing, almost big enough for a giant,—such was the barn at Hartley Farm; as pleasant a place, Hilda thought, as she had ever seen.

"Waal, Huldy, I'll leave ye heer," said the farmer; "ye kin find yer way home, I reckon."

"Oh, yes, indeed!" said Hilda. "But stop one moment, please, Farmer Hartley. I want to know—will you please—may I teach Bubble Chirk a little?" The farmer gave a low whistle of surprise; but Hilda went on eagerly: "I found him studying, this morning, while he was weeding the garden,—oh! studying so hard, and yet not neglecting his work for a minute. He seems a very bright boy, and it is a pity he should not have a good education. Could you spare him, do you think, for an hour every day?" She stopped, while the farmer looked at her with a merry twinkle in his eye.

"You teach Bubble Chirk!" he said. "Why, what would your fine friends say to that, Miss Huldy? Bubble ain't nothin' but a common farm-boy, if he is bright; an' I ain't denyin' that he is."

"I don't know what they would say," said Hildegarde, blushing hotly, "and I don't care, either! I know what mamma would do in my place; and so do you, Farmer Hartley!" she added, with a little touch of indignation.

"Waal, I reckon I do!" said Farmer Hartley. "And I know who looks like her mother, this minute, though I never thought she would. Yes!" he said, more seriously, "you shall teach Bubble Chirk, my gal; and it's my belief 'twill bring you a blessin' as well as him. Ye are yer mother's darter, after all. Shall I give ye a swing now, before I go; or are ye too big to swing!"

"I—don't—know!" said Hildegarde, eying the swing wistfully. "Am I too big, I wonder?"

"Yer ma warn't, when she was here three weeks ago!" said the farmer. "She just sot heer and took a good solid swing, for the sake of old times, she said."

"Then I will take one for the sake of new times!" cried Hilda, running to the swing and seating herself on its broad, roomy seat. "For the sake of this new time, which I know is going to be a happy one, give me three good pushes, please, Farmer Hartley, and then I can take care of myself."

One! two! three! up goes Queen Hildegarde, up and up, among the dusty, cobwebby sunbeams, which settle like a crown upon her fair head. Down with a rush, through the sweet, hay-scented air; then up again, startling the swallows from under the eaves, and making the staid and conservative old hens frantic with anxiety. Up and down, in broad, free sweeps, growing slower now, as the farmer left her and went to his work. How perfect it was! Did the world hold anything else so delightful as swinging in a barn? She began to sing, for pure joy, a little song that her mother had made for her when she was a little child, and used to swing in the garden at home. And Farmer Hartley, with his hand on the brown heifer's back, paused with a smile and a sigh as he heard the girl's sweet fresh voice ring out gladly from the old barn. This was the song she sang:—

28

If I were a fairy king
(Swinging high, swinging low),
I would give to you a ring
(Swinging, oh!)
With a diamond set so bright
That the shining of its light
Should make morning of the night
(Swinging high, swinging low)—
Should make morning of the night
(Swinging, oh!).

On each ringlet as it fell
(Swinging high, swinging low)
I would tie a golden bell
(Swinging, oh!);
And the golden bells would chime
In a little merry rhyme,
In the merry morning time
(Swinging high, swinging low)—
In the happy morning time
(Swinging, oh!).

You should wear a satin gown
(Swinging high, swinging low),
All with ribbons falling down
(Swinging, oh!).
And your little twinkling feet,
O my Pretty and my Sweet!
Should be shod with silver neat
(Swinging high, swinging low)—
Shod with silver slippers neat
(Swinging, oh!).

But I'm not a fairy, Pet
(Swinging high, swinging low),
Am not even a king, as yet
(Swinging, oh!).
So all that I can do
Is to kiss your little shoe,
And to make a queen of you
(Swinging high, swinging low),
Make a fairy queen of you
(Swinging, oh!).
CHAPTER VI.

HARTLEY'S GLEN.

How many girls, among all the girls who may read this little book, have seen with their own eyes Hartley's Glen? Not one, perhaps, save Brynhild and the Rosicrucian, for whom the book is written. But the others must try to see it with my eyes, for it is a fair place and a sweet as any on earth. Behind the house, and just under the brow of the little hill that shelters it, a narrow path dips down to the right, and goes along for a bit, with a dimpled clover-meadow on the one hand, and a stone wall, all warm with golden and red-brown lichens, on the other. Follow this, and you come to a little gateway, beyond which is a thick plantation of larches, with one grim old red cedar keeping watch over them. If he regards you favorably, you may pass on, down the narrow path that winds among the larches, whose feathery finger-tips brush your cheek and try to hold you back, as if they willed not that you should go farther, to see the wonders which they can never behold.

But you leave them behind, and come out into the sunshine, in a little green glade which might be the ballroom of the fairy queen. On your right, gleaming through clumps of alder and black birch, is a pond,—the home of cardinal flowers and gleaming jewel-weed; a little farther on, a thicket of birch and maple, from which comes a musical sound of falling water. Follow this sound, keeping to the path, which winds away to the left. Stop! now you may step aside for a moment, and part the heavy hanging branches, and look, where the water falls over a high black wall, into a sombre pool, shut in by fantastic rocks, and shaded from all sunshine by a dense fringe of trees. This is the milldam, and the pond above is no natural one, but the enforced repose and outspreading of a merry brown brook, which now shows its true nature, and escaping from the gloomy pool, runs scolding and foaming down through a wilderness of rocks and trees. You cannot follow it there,—though I have often done so in my barefoot days,—so come back to the path again. There are pines overhead now, and the ground is slippery with the fallen needles, and the air is sweet—ah! how sweet!—with their warm fragrance. See! here is the old mill itself, now disused and falling to decay. Here the path becomes a little precipice, and you must scramble as best you can down two or three rough steps, and round the corner of the ruined mill. This is a millstone, this great round thing like a granite cheese, half buried in the ground; and here is another, which makes a comfortable seat, if you are tired.

But there is a fairer resting-place beyond. Round this one more corner, now, and down,—carefully, carefully!—down this long stairway, formed of rough slabs of stone laid one below the other. Shut your eyes now for a moment, and let me lead you forward by the hand. And now—now open the eyes wide, wide, and look about you. In front, and under the windows of the old mill, the water comes foaming and rushing down over a rocky fall some sixty feet high, and leaps merrily into a second pool. No sombre, black gulf this, like the one above, but a lovely open circle, half in broad sunshine, half dappled with the fairy shadows of the boughs and ferns that bend lovingly over it. So the little brook is no longer angry, but mingles lovingly with the deep water of the pool, and then runs laughing and singing along the glen on its way down to the sea. On one side of this glen the bank rises abruptly some eighty feet, its sides clothed with sturdy birches which cling as best they may to the rocky steep. On the other stretches the little valley, a narrow strip of land, but with turf as fine as the Queen's lawn, and trees that would proudly grace Her Majesty's park,—tall Norway firs, raising their stately forms and pointing their long dark fingers sternly at the intruders on their solitude; graceful birches; and here and there a whispering larch or a nodding pine. The other wall of the valley, or glen, is less precipitous, and its sides are densely wooded, and fringed with barberry bushes and climbing eglantine.

30

And between these two banks, and over this green velvet carpet, and among these dark fir-trees,—ah! how the sun shines. Nowhere else in the whole land does he shine so sweetly, for he knows that his time there is short, and that the high banks will shut him out from that green, pleasant place long before he must say good-night to the more common-place fields and hill-sides. So here his beams rest right lovingly, making royal show of gold on the smooth grass, and of diamonds on the running water, and of opals and topazes and beryls where the wave comes curling over the little fall.

And now, amid all this pomp and play of sun and of summer, what is this dash of blue that makes a strange, though not a discordant, note in our harmony of gold and green? And what is that round, whitish object which is bobbing up and down with such singular energy? Why, the blue is Hildegarde's dress, if you must know; and the whitish object is the head of Zerubbabel Chirk, scholar and devotee; and the energy with which said head is bobbing is the energy of determination and of study. Hilda and Bubble have made themselves extremely comfortable under the great ash-tree which stands in the centre of the glen. The teacher has curled herself up against the roots of the tree, and has a piece of work in her hands; but her eyes are wandering dreamily over the lovely scene before her, and she looks as if she were really too comfortable to move even a finger. The scholar lies at her feet, face downwards, his chin propped on his hands, his head bobbing up and down. The silence is only broken by the noise of the waterfall and the persistent chirping of some very cheerful little bird.

Presently the boy raised his head and cried joyfully, "I've fetched him, Miss Hildy! I know it, now, jest like pie!" Whereupon he stood up, and assuming a military attitude, submitted to a severe geographical catechising, and came off with flying colors.

"That was a very good recitation," said Hilda, approvingly, as she laid the book down. "You shall have another ballad to-day as a reward. But, Bubble," she added, rather seriously, "I do wish you would not use so much slang. It is so senseless! Now what did you mean by saying 'just like pie,' in speaking of your lesson just now?"

"Oh! come now, Miss Hildy!" said Bubble, bashfully, "the' ain't no use in your tellin' me you don't know what pie is."

"Of course I know what pie is, you silly boy!" said Hilda, laughing. "But what has pie to do with your geography lesson?"

"That's so!" murmured the boy, apologetically. "That's a fact, ain't it! I won't say 'like pie' no more; I'll say 'like blazes,' instead."

"You needn't say 'like' anything!" cried Hilda, laughing again; "just say, I know my lesson 'well,' or 'thoroughly.' There are plenty of real words, Bubble, that have as much meaning as the slang ones, and often a great deal more."

"That's so," said Bubble, with an air of deep conviction. "I'll try not to talk no more slang, Miss Hildy. I will, I swan!"

"But, Bubble, you must not say 'I swan' either; that is abominable slang."

31

Bubble looked very blank. "Why, what shall I say?" he asked, simply. "Pink won't let me say 'I swow,' 'cause it's vulgar; an' if I say 'by' anything, Ma says it's swearin',—an' I can't swear, nohow!"

"Of course not," said Hilda. "But why must you say anything, Bubble,—anything of that sort, I mean?"

"Oh!" said the boy, "I d' 'no 's I kin say ezackly why, Miss Hildy; but—but—wal, I swan! I mean, I—I don't mean I swan—but—there now! You see how 'tis, Miss Hildy. Things don't seem to hev no taste to 'em, without you say somethin'."

"Let me think," said Hilda. "Perhaps I can think of something that will sound better."

"I might say, 'Gee Whittekers!'" suggested Bubble, brightening up a little. "I know some fellers as says that."

"I don't think that would do," replied Hilda, decidedly. "What does it mean?"

"Don't mean nothing as I knows on," said the boy; "but it sounds kind o' hahnsome, don't it?"

Hilda shook her head with a smile. She did not think "Gee Whittekers" a "hahnsome" expression.

"Bubble," she said after a few moments' reflection, during which her scholar watched her anxiously, "I have an idea. If you must say 'something,' beside what you actually have to say, let it be something that will remind you of your lessons; then it may help you to remember them. Instead of Gee—what is it?—Gee Whittekers, say Geography, or Spelling, or Arithmetic; and instead of 'I swan,' say 'I study!' What do you think of this plan?"

"Fustrate!" exclaimed Bubble, nodding his head enthusiastically. "I like fustrate! Geography! Why, that sounds just like pie! I—I don't mean that, Miss Hildy. I didn't mean to say it, nohow! It kind o' slipped out, ye know." Bubble paused, and hung his head in much confusion.

"Never mind!" said Hilda, kindly. "Of course you cannot make the change all at once, Bubble. But little by little, if you really think about it, you will bring it about. Next week," she added, "I think we must begin upon grammar. You are doing very well indeed in spelling and geography, and pretty well in arithmetic; but your grammar, Bubble, is simply frightful."

"Be it?" said Bubble, resignedly. "I want to know!"

"And now," said the young instructress, rising, and shaking out her crumpled frock, "that is enough for to-day, Bubble. We must be going home soon; but first, I want to take

32

a peep at the lower part of the old mill, that you told me about yesterday. You have been in there, you say? And how did you get in?"

"I'll show ye!" cried Bubble, springing up with alacrity, and leading the way towards the mill. "I'll show ye the very place, Miss Hildy. 'Tain't easy to get in, and 'tain't no place for a lady, nohow; but I kin git in, jist like—like 'rithmetic!"

"Bravo, Bubble!" said Hilda, laughing merrily. "That is very well for a beginning. How long is it since the mill was used?" she asked, looking up at the frowning walls of rough, dark stone, covered with moss and lichens.

"Farmer Hartley's gran'f'ther was the last miller," replied Bubble Chirk. "My father used to say he could just remember him, standin' at the mill-door, all white with flour, an' rubbin' his hands and laughin', jes' the way Farmer does. He was a good miller, father said, an' made the mill pay well. But his eldest son, that kem after him, warn't no great shakes, an' he let the mill go to wrack and ruin, an' jes' stayed on the farm. An' then he died, an' Cap'n Hartley came (that's the farmer's father, ye know), an' he was kind o' crazy, and didn't care about the mill either, an' so there it stayed.

"This way, Miss Hildy!" added the boy, breaking off suddenly, and plunging into the tangled thicket of shrubs and brambles that hid the base of the mill. "Thar! ye see that hole? That's whar I get in. Wait till I clear away the briers a bit! Thar! now ye kin look in."

The "hole" was a square opening, a couple of feet from the ground, and large enough for a person of moderate size to creep through. Hildegarde stooped down and looked in. At first she saw nothing but utter blackness; but presently her eyes became accustomed to the place, and the feeble light which struggled in past her through the opening, revealed strange objects which rose here and there from the vast pit of darkness,—fragments of rusty iron, bent and twisted into unearthly shapes; broken beams, their jagged ends sticking out like stiffly pointing fingers; cranks, and bits of hanging chain; and on the side next the water, a huge wheel, rising apparently out of the bowels of the earth, since the lower part of it was invisible. A cold, damp air seemed to rise from the earth. Hilda shivered and drew back, looking rather pale. "What a dreadful place!" she cried. "It looks like a dungeon of the Inquisition. I think you were very brave to go in there, Bubble. I am sure I should not dare to go; it looks so spectral and frightful."

"Hy Peters stumped me to go," said Bubble, simply, "so o' course I went. Most of the boys dassent. And it ain't bad, after the fust time. They do say it's haunted; but I ain't never seed nothin'."

"Haunted!" cried Hilda, drawing back still farther from the black opening. "By—by what, Bubble?"

"Cap'n's ghost!" replied the boy. "He used to go rooklin' round in there when he was alive, folks say, and some thinks his sperit haunts there now."

"Oh, nonsense!" said Hildegarde, with a laugh which did not sound quite natural. "Of course you don't believe any such foolishness as that, Bubble. But what did the old—

old gentleman—want there when he was alive? I can't imagine any one going in there for pleasure."

"Dunno, I'm sure!" replied Bubble. "Father, he come down here one day, after blackberries, when he was a boy. He hearn a noise in there, an' went an' peeked in, an' there was the ol' Cap'n pokin' about with his big stick in the dirt. He looked up an' saw father, an' came at him with his stick up, roarin' like a mad bull, father said. An' he cut an' run, father did, an' he hearn the ol' Cap'n laughin' after him as if he'd have a fit. Crazy as a loon, I reckon the Cap'n was, though none of his folks thought so, Ma says."

He let the wild briers fly back about the gloomy opening, and they stepped back on the smooth greensward again. Ah, how bright and warm the sunshine was, after that horrible black pit! Hilda shivered again at the thought of it, and then laughed at her own cowardice. She turned and gazed at the waterfall, creaming and curling over the rocks, and making such a merry, musical jest of its tumble into the pool. "Oh, lovely, lovely!" she cried, kissing her hand to it. "Bubble, do you know that Hartley's Glen is without exception the most beautiful place in the world?"

"No, miss! Be it really?" asked Zerubbabel, seriously. "I allays thought 'twas kind of a sightly gully, but I didn't know't was all that."

"Well, it is," said Hilda. "It is all that, and more; and I love it! But now, Bubble," she added, "we must make haste, for the farmer will be wanting you, and I have a dozen things to do before tea."

"Yes, miss," said Bubble, but without his usual alacrity.

Hilda saw a look of disappointment in his honest blue eyes, and asked what was the matter. "I ain't had my ballid!" said Zerubbabel, sadly.

"Why, you poor lad, so you haven't!" said Hildegarde. "But you shall have it; I will tell it to you as we walk back to the farm. Which one will you have,—or shall I tell you a new one?"

The blue eyes sparkled with the delight of anticipation. "Oh, please!" he cried; "the one about the bold Buckle-oh!"

Hilda laughed merrily. "The bauld Buccleugh?" she repeated. "Oh! you mean 'Kinmont Willie.' Yes, indeed, you shall have that. It is one of my favorite ballads, and I am glad you like it."

"Oh, I tell yer!" cried Bubble. "When he whangs the table, and says do they think his helmet's an old woman's bunnit, an' all the rest of it,—I tell ye that's some, Miss Hildy!"

"You have the spirit of the verse, Bubble," said Hilda, laughing softly; "but the words are not quite right." And she repeated the splendid, ringing words of Buccleugh's indignant outcry:

"Oh! is my basnet a widow's curch,

34

Or my lance a wand o' the willow-tree,
Or my arm a lady's lily hand,
That an English lord should lightly me?

"And have they ta'en him, Kinmont Willie,
Against the truce of Border tide,
And forgotten that the bauld Buccleugh
Is warden here o' the Scottish side?

"And have they e'en ta'en him, Kinmont Willie,
Withouten either dread or fear,
And forgotten that the bauld Buccleugh
Can back a steed or shake a spear?"

Zerubbabel Chirk fairly danced up and down in his excitement "Oh! but begin again at the beginning, please, Miss Hildy," he cried.

So Hilda, nothing loth, began at the beginning; and as they walked homeward, recited the whole of the noble old ballad, which if any girl-reader does not know, she may find it in any collection of Scottish ballads.

"And the best of it is, Bubble," said Hilda, "that it is all true,—every word of it; or nearly every word."

"I'll bet it is!" cried Bubble, still much excited. "They couldn't make lies sound like that, ye know! You kind o' know it's true, and it goes right through yer, somehow. When did it happen, Miss Hildy?"

"Oh! a long time ago," said Hildegarde; "near the end of the sixteenth century. I forget just the very year, but it was in the reign of Queen Elizabeth. She was very angry at Buccleugh's breaking into Carlisle Castle, which was an English castle, you see, and carrying off Lord Scroope's prisoner; and she sent word to King James of Scotland that he must give up Buccleugh to her to punish as she saw fit. King James refused at first, for he said that Lord Scroope had been the first to break the truce by carrying off Kinmont Willie in time of peace; but at length he was obliged to yield, for Queen Elizabeth was very powerful, and always would have her own way. So the 'bauld Buccleugh' was sent to London and brought before the great, haughty English queen. But he was just as haughty as she, and was not a bit afraid of her. She looked down on him from her throne (she was very stately, you know, and she wore a crown, and a great stiff ruff, and her dress was all covered with gold and precious stones), and asked him how he dared to undertake such a desperate and presumptuous enterprise. And Buccleugh—O Bubble, I always liked this so much!—Buccleugh just looked her full in the face, and said, 'What is it a man dare not do?' Now Queen Elizabeth liked nothing so much as a brave man, and this bold answer pleased her. She turned to one of her ministers and said, 'With ten thousand such men our brother in Scotland might shake the firmest throne in Europe.' And so she let him go, just because he was so brave and so handsome."

Bubble Chirk drew a long breath, and his eyes flashed. "I wish't I'd ben alive then!" he said.

"Why, Bubble?" asked Hilda, much amused; "what would you have done?"

"I'd ha' killed Lord Scroope!" he cried,—"him and the hull kit of 'em. Besides," he added, "I'd like t' ha' lived then jest ter see him,—jest ter see the bold Buckle-oh; that's what I call a man!" And Queen Hildegardis fully agreed with him.

They had nearly reached the house when the boy asked: "If that king was her brother, why did she treat him so kind o' ugly? My sister don't act that way."

"What—oh, you mean Queen Elizabeth!" said Hilda, laughing. "King James was not her brother, Bubble. They were cousins, but nothing more."

"You said she said 'brother,'" persisted the boy.

"So I did," replied Hilda. "You see, it was the fashion, and is still, for kings and queens to call each other brother and sister, whether they were really related to each other or not."

"But I thought they was always fightin'," objected Bubble. "I've got a hist'ry book to home, an' in that it says they fit like time whenever they got a chance."

"So they did," said Hilda. "But they called each other 'our royal brother' and 'our beloved sister;' and they were always paying each other fine compliments, and saying how much they loved each other, even in the middle of a war, when they were fighting as hard as they could."

"Humph!" said Bubble, "nice kind o folks they must ha' been. Well, I must go, Miss Hildy," he added, reluctantly. "I've had a splendid time, an' I'm real obleeged to ye. I sh'll try to larn that story by heart, 'bout the bold Buckle-oh. I want to tell it to Pink! She'd like it—oh, my! wouldn't she like it, jest like—I mean jest like spellin'! Good by, Miss Hildy!" And Bubble ran off to bring home the cows, his little heart swelling high with scorn of kings and queens, and with a fervor of devotion to Walter Scott, first lord of Buccleugh.

CHAPTER VII.

PINK CHIRK.

One lovely morning Hildegarde stood at the back door, feeding the fowls. She wore her brown gingham frock with the yellow daisies on it, and the daisy-wreathed hat, and in her hands she held a great yellow bowl full of yellow corn. So bright a picture she made that Farmer Hartley, driving the oxen afield, stopped for pure pleasure to look at her. Around her the ducks and hens were fighting and squabbling, quacking, clucking, and gobbling, and she flung the corn in golden showers on their heads and backs, making them nearly frantic with greedy anxiety.

"SHE FLUNG THE CORN IN GOLDEN SHOWERS ON THEIR HEADS."
"SHE FLUNG THE CORN IN GOLDEN SHOWERS ON THEIR HEADS."

36

"Wal, Huldy," said the farmer, leaning against Bright's massive side, "you look pooty slick in that gown, I must say. I reckon thar ain't no sech gown as that on Fifth Avenoo, hey?"

"Indeed, I don't believe there is, Farmer Hartley," replied Hilda, laughing merrily; "at least I never saw one like it. It is pretty, I think, and so comfortable! And where are you going this morning with the mammoths?"

"Down to the ten-acre lot," replied the farmer. "The men are makin' hay thar to-day. Jump into the riggin' and come along," he added. "Ye kin hev a little ride, an' see the hay-makin'. Pooty sight 'tis, to my thinkin'."

"May I?" cried Hilda, eagerly. "I am sure these fowls have had enough. Go away now, you greedy creatures! There, you shall have all there is!" and she emptied the bowl over the astonished dignitaries of the barn-yard, laid it down on the settle in the porch, and jumped gayly into the "rigging," as the great hay-cart was called.

"Haw, Bright! hoish, Star!" said the farmer, touching one and then the other of the great black oxen lightly with his goad. The huge beasts swayed from side to side, and finally succeeded in getting themselves and the cart in motion, while the farmer walked leisurely beside them, tapping and poking them occasionally, and talking to them in that mystic language which only oxen and their drivers understand. Down the sweet country lane they went, with the willows hanging over them, and the daisies and buttercups and meadow-sweet running riot all over the banks. Hilda stood up in the cart and pulled off twigs from the willows as she passed under them, and made garlands, which the farmer obediently put over the oxen's necks. She hummed little snatches of song, and chatted gayly with her kind old host; for the world was very fair, and her heart was full of summer and sunshine.

"And have you always lived here, Farmer Hartley?" she asked. "All your life, I mean?"

"No, not all my life," replied the farmer, "though pooty nigh it. I was ten year old when my uncle died, and father left sea-farin', and kem home to the farm to live. Before that we'd lived in different places, movin' round, like. We was at sea a good deal, sailin' with father when he went on pleasant voyages, to the West Indies, or sich. But sence then I ain't ben away much. I don't seem to find no pleasanter place than the old farm, somehow."

"I don't believe there is any pleasanter place in the world!" said Hilda, warmly. "I am sure I have never been so happy anywhere as I have here."

Farmer Hartley looked up with a twinkle in his eye. "Ye've changed yer views some, Huldy, hain't ye, since the fust day ye kem heer? I didn't never think, then, as I'd be givin' you rides in the hay-riggin', sech a fine young lady as you was."

Hilda gave him an imploring glance, while the blood mounted to her temples. "Please, Farmer Hartley," she said in a low voice, "please try to forget that first day. It isn't my views that have changed," she added, "it is I myself. I don't—I really don't think I am the same girl who came here a month ago."

"No, my gal," said the farmer, heartily, "I don't think ye are." He walked along in silence for a few minutes, and then said, "'Tis curus how folks kin sometimes change 'emselves, one way or the other. 'Tain't so with critturs; 't least so fur's I've observed. The way they're born, that way they'll stay. Now look at them oxen! When they was young steers, hardly more'n calves, I began to train them critturs. An' from the very fust go-off they tuk their cue an' stuck to it. Star, thar, would lay out, and shake his head, an' pull for all he was wuth, as if there was nothin' in the world to do but pull; and Bright, he'd wait till Star was drawin' good an' solid, an' then he'd as much as say, 'Oh! you kin pull all that, kin ye? Well, stick to it, my boy, an' I'll manage to trifle along with the rest o' the load.' Wo-hoish, Star! haw, Bright! git up, ye old humbug! You're six year old now, an' you ain't changed a mite in four years, though I've drove you stiddy, and tried to spare the other every time."

The green lane broke off suddenly, and such a blaze of sunlight flashed upon them that Hilda involuntarily raised her hand to shield her eyes. The great meadow lay open before them, an undulating plain of gold. The haycocks looked dull and gray-green upon it; but where the men were tossing the hay with their long wooden rakes, it flashed pale-golden in the sunlight, and filled the air with flying gleams. Also the air was filled with the sweetness of the hay, and every breath was a delight. Hilda stood speechless with pleasure, and the old farmer watched her glowing face with kindly gratification.

"Pooty sightly, ain't it?" he said. And then, in a graver tone, and removing his battered straw hat, "I don't never seem to see the glory of the Lord no plainer than in a hay-field, a day like this. Yes, sir! if a man can't be a Christian on a farm in summer, he can't be it nowhere. Amen!" and Farmer Hartley put on his hat and proceeded straightway to business. "Now, Huldy," he said, "here ye be! I'm goin' to load up this riggin', an' ye kin stay round here a spell, if ye like, an' run home when ye like. Ye kin find the way, I reckon?"

"Oh, yes!" said Hilda; "yes, indeed! But I shall stay here for a while, and watch you. And mayn't I toss the hay too a little?"

But her courage failed when she found that to do this she must mingle with the crowd of strange haymakers; and besides, among them she saw the clumsy form and shock head of Caliban, as she had secretly named the clownish and surly nephew of her good host. This fellow was the one bitter drop in Hilda's cup. Everything else she had learned to like, in the month which had passed since she came to Hartley's Glen. The farmer and his wife she loved as they deserved to be loved. The little maidservant was her adoring slave, and secretly sewed her boot-buttons on, and mended her stockings, as some small return for the lessons in crochet and fancy knitting that she had received from the skilful white fingers which were a perpetual marvel to her. But Simon Hartley remained what she had at first thought him,—a sullen, boorish churl. He was a malevolent churl too, Hildegarde thought; indeed she was sure of it. She had several times seen his eyes fixed on his uncle with a look of positive hatred; and though Farmer Hartley was persistently kind and patient with him, trying often to draw him into conversation, and make him join in the pleasant evening talks which they all enjoyed, his efforts were unsuccessful. The fellow came in, gobbled his food, and then went off, if his work was over, to hide himself in his own room. Hilda was quite sure that Nurse Lucy liked this oaf no better than she herself did, though the good woman never spoke impatiently or unkindly to him,—and indeed it would be difficult for any one to like him, she thought, except possibly his own mother.

Our Queen took presently her seat on a right royal throne of fragrant hay, and gave herself up to the full delight of the summer morning, and of the "Field of the Cloth of Gold," as she had instantly named the shining yellow plain, which more prosaic souls knew as "the ten-acre lot." The hay rustled pleasantly as she nestled down in it, and made a little penthouse over her head, to keep off the keen, hot sun-arrows. There was a great oak-tree too, which partly shaded this favored haycock, and on one of its branches a squirrel came running out, and then sat up and looked at Hildegarde with bright, inquisitive eyes. A maiden, all brown and gold, on a golden haycock! What strange apparition was this? Had she come for acorns? Did she know about the four young ones in the snug little house in the hollow just above the first branch! Perhaps—dreadful thought!—she had heard of the marvellous beauty of the four young ones, and had come to steal them. "Chip!" whisk! and Madam Squirrel was off up the branch like a streak of brown lightning, with its tail up.

Hilda laughed at the squirrel's alarm, and then turned her attention to a large green grasshopper who seemed to demand it. He had alighted on her knee, and now proceeded to exhibit his different points before her admiring gaze with singular gravity and deliberation. First he slowly opened his wings, to show the delicate silvery gauze of the under-wings; then as slowly closed them, demonstrating the perfect fit of his whole wing-costume and the harmony of its colors. He next extended one leg, calling her attention to its remarkable length and muscular proportions. Then, lest she should think he had but one, he extended the other; and then gave a vigorous hop with both of them, to show her that he did not really need wings, but could get on perfectly well without them. Finally he rubbed himself all over with his long antennæ, and then, pointing them full at her, and gazing at her with calm and dispassionate eyes, he said plainly enough: "And now, Monster, what have you to show me?"

Hildegarde was wondering how she could best dispel the scorn with which this majestic insect evidently regarded her, when suddenly something new appeared on her gown,—something black, many-legged, hairy, most hideous; something which ran swiftly but stealthily, with a motion which sent a thrill of horror through her veins. She started up with a little shriek, shaking off the unlucky spider as if it had been the Black Death in concrete. Then she looked round with flaming cheeks, to see if her scream had been heard by the hay-makers. No, they were far away, and too busy to take heed of her. But the charm was broken. Queen Hildegarde had plenty of courage of a certain sort, but she could not face a spider. The golden throne had become a "siege perilous," and she abdicated in favor of the grasshopper and his black and horrent visitor.

What should she do now? The charm of the morning had made her idle and drowsy, and she did not feel like going home to help Nurse Lucy in making the butter, though she often did so with right good-will. She looked dreamily around, her eyes wandering here and there over the great meadow and the neat stone walls which bounded it. Presently she spied the chimneys and part of the red roof of a little cottage which peeped from a thick clump of trees just beyond the wall. Who lived in that cottage, Hilda wondered. Why should she not go and see? She was very thirsty, and there she might get a glass of water. Oh! perhaps it was Bubble's cottage, where he and his mother and his sister Pink lived. Now she thought of it, Bubble had told her that he lived "over beyont the ten-acre lot;" of course this must be the place. Slowly she walked across the meadow and climbed the wall, wondering a good deal about the people whom she was going to see. She had often meant to ask Bubble more about his sister with the queer name; but the lesson-hour was so short, and there were always so many questions for Bubble to ask and for her to answer besides the regular lesson, that she always forgot it till too late. Pink Chirk! what could a girl be like with such a name as that? Hilda fancied her a stout, buxom maiden, with very red cheeks and very black eyes—yes, certainly, the eyes must be black! Her hair—well, one could not be so sure about her hair; but there was no doubt about her wearing a pink dress and a blue checked apron. And she must be smiling, bustling, and energetic. Yes! Hilda had the picture of her complete in her mind. She wondered that this active, stirring girl never came up to the farm; but of course she must have a great deal of work to do at home.

By this time Hildegarde had reached the cottage; and after a moment's hesitation she knocked softly at the green-painted door. No one came to open the door, but presently she heard a clear, pleasant voice from within saying, "Open the door and come in, please!" Following this injunction, she entered the cottage and found herself directly in the sitting-room, and face to face with its occupant. This was a girl of her own age, or perhaps a year older, who sat in a wheeled chair by the window. She was very fair, with almost flaxen hair, and frank, pleasant blue eyes. She was very pale, very thin; the hands that lay on her lap were almost transparent; but—she wore a pink calico dress and a blue checked apron. Who could this be? and whoever it was, why did she sit still when a visitor and a stranger came in? The pale girl made no attempt to rise, but she met Hilda's look of surprise and inquiry with a smile which broke like sunshine over her face, making it for the moment positively beautiful. "How do you do?" she said, holding out her thin hand. "I am sure you must be Miss Hilda Graham, and I am Bubble's sister Pink.

"THE PALE GIRL MADE NO ATTEMPT TO RISE."
"THE PALE GIRL MADE NO ATTEMPT TO RISE."
"Please sit down," she added. "I am so very glad to see you. I have wanted again and again to thank you for all your kindness to my Bubble, but I didn't know when I should have a chance. Did Bubble show you the way?"

Hildegarde was so astonished, so troubled, so dismayed that she hardly knew what she was saying or doing. She took the slender fingers in her own for an instant, and then sat down, saying hastily: "Oh, no! I—I found my way alone. I was not sure of its being your cottage, though I thought it must be from what Bubble told me." She paused; and then, unable to keep back longer the words which sprang to her lips, she said: "I fear you have been ill, you are so pale. I hope it has not been serious. Bubble did not tell me—"

Pink Chirk looked up with her bright, sweet smile. "Oh, no! I have not been ill," she said. "I am always like this. I cannot walk, you know, but I am very well indeed."

"You cannot walk?" stammered Hilda.

40

The girl saw her look of horror, and a faint color stole into her wan cheek. "Did not Bubble tell you?" she asked, gently; and then, as Hilda shook her head, "It is such a matter of course to him," she said; "he never thinks about it, I suppose, dear little fellow. I was run over when I was three years old, and I have never been able to walk since."

Hildegarde could not speak. The thought of anything so dreadful, so overwhelming as this, coming so suddenly, too, upon her, seemed to take away her usually ready speech, and she was dumb, gazing at the cheerful face before her with wide eyes of pity and wonderment. But Pink Chirk did not like to be pitied, as a rule; and she almost laughed at her visitor's horror-stricken face.

"You mustn't look so!" she cried. "It's very kind of you to be sorry, but it isn't as if I were really ill, you know. I can almost stand on one foot,—that is, I can bear enough weight on it to get from my bed to my chair without help. That is a great thing! And then when I am once in my chair, why I can go almost anywhere. Farmer Hartley gave me this chair," she added, looking down at it, and patting the arm tenderly, as if it were a living friend; "isn't it a beauty?"

It was a pretty chair, made of cherry wood, with cushions of gay-flowered chintz; and Hilda, finding her voice again, praised it warmly. "This is its summer dress," said Pink, her eyes sparkling with pleasure. "Underneath, the cushions are covered with soft crimson cloth, oh, so pretty, and so warm-looking! I am always glad when it's time to take the chintz covers off. And yet I am always glad to put them on again," she added, "for the chintz is pretty too, I think: and besides, I know then that summer is really come."

"You like summer best?" asked Hilda.

"Oh, yes!" she replied. "In winter, of course, I can't go out; and sometimes it seems a little long, when Bubble is away all day,—not very, you know, but just a little. But in summer, oh, then I am so happy! I can go all round the place by myself, and sit out in the garden, and feed the chickens, and take care of the flowers. And then on Sunday Bubble always gives me a good ride along the road. My chair moves very easily,—only see!" She gave a little push, and propelled herself half way across the little room.

At this moment the inner door opened, and Mrs. Chirk appeared,—a slender, anxious-looking woman, with hair prematurely gray. She greeted Hilda with nervous cordiality, and thanked her earnestly for her kindness to Zerubbabel. "He ain't the same boy, Miss Graham," she said, "sence you begun givin' him lessons. He used to fret and worrit 'cause there warn't no school, and he couldn't ha' gone to it if there was. Pinkrosia learned him what she could; but we hain't many books, you see. But now! why that boy comes into the house singin' and spoutin' poetry at the top of his lungs,—jest as happy as a kitten with a spool. What was that he was shoutin' this mornin', Pinkrosia, when he scairt the old black hen nigh to death?"

"'Charge for the golden lilies! Upon them with the lance!'" murmured Pink, with a smile.

"Yes, that was it!" said Mrs. Chirk. "He was lookin' out of the window and pumpin' at the same time, an' spoutin' them verses too. And all of a sudden he cries out, 'Ther's

41

the brood of dark My Hen, scratchin' up the sweet peas. Upon them with the lance!' And he lets go the pump-handle, and it flies up and hits the shelf and knocks off two plates and a cup, and Bubble, he's off with the mop-handle, chasin' the old black hen and makin' believe run her through, till she e'enamost died of fright. Well, there, it give me a turn; it reelly did!" She paused rather sadly, seeing that her hearers were both overcome with laughter.

"I—I am very sorry, Mrs. Chirk, that the plates were broken," said Hilda; "but it must have been extremely funny. Poor old hen! she must have been frightened, certainly. Do you know," she added, "I think Bubble is a remarkably bright boy. I am very sure that he will make a name for himself, if only he can have proper training."

"Presume likely!" said Mrs. Chirk, with melancholy satisfaction. "His father was a real smart man. There warn't no better hayin' hand in the county than Loammi Chirk. And I'm in hopes Zerubbabel will do as well, for he has a good friend in Farmer Hartley; no boy couldn't have a better."

Eminence in the profession of "haying" was not precisely what Hilda had meant; but she said nothing.

"And my poor girl here," Mrs. Chirk continued after a pause, "she sets in her cheer hay-times and other times. You've heard of her misfortune, Miss Graham?"

Pink interposed quickly with a little laugh, though her brows contracted slightly, as if with pain. "Oh, yes, Mother dear!" she said; "Miss Graham has heard all about me, and knows what a very important person I am. But where is the yarn that I was to wind for you? I thought you wanted to begin weaving this afternoon."

"Oh!" exclaimed Hildegarde. "Never mind the yarn just now, Pink! I want to give you a little ride before I go back to the farm. May she go, Mrs. Chirk? It is such a beautiful day, I am sure the air will do her good. Would you like it, Pink?"

Pink looked up with a flush of pleasure on her pale cheek. "Oh," she said, "would I like it! But it's too much for you to do, Miss Graham."

"An' with that beautiful dress on too!" cried Mrs. Chirk. "You'd get it dusty on the wheel, I'm afraid. I don't think—"

"Oh yes, you do!" cried Hilda, gayly, pushing the chair towards the door. "Bring her hat, please, Mrs. Chirk. I always have my own way!" she added, with a touch of the old imperiousness, "and I have quite set my heart on this."

Mrs. Chirk meekly brought a straw sun-bonnet, and Hilda tied its strings under Pink's chin, every fibre within her mutely protesting against its extreme ugliness. "She shall not wear that again," said she to herself, "if I can help it." But the sweet pale face looked out so joyously from the dingy yellow tunnel that the stern young autocrat relented. "After all, what does it matter?" she thought. "She would look like an angel, even with a real coal-scuttle on her head." And then she laughed at the thought of a black japanned scuttle crowning those fair locks; and Pink laughed because Hilda laughed; and so they both went laughing out into the sunshine.

CHAPTER VIII.

THE LETTER.

"Nurse Lucy," said Hildegarde that evening, as they sat in the porch after tea, "why have you never told me about Pink Chirk,—about her being a cripple, I mean? I had no idea of it till I went to see her to-day. How terrible it is!"

"I wonder that I haven't told you, dear!" replied Nurse Lucy, placidly. "I suppose I am so used to Pink as she is, I forget that she ever was like other people. She is a dear, good child,—his 'sermon,' Jacob calls her. He says that whenever he feels impatient or put out, he likes to go down and look at Pink, and hear her talk. 'It takes the crook right out of me!' he says. Poor Jacob!"

"But how did it happen?" asked Hilda. "She says she was only three years when she—Oh, think of it, Nurse Lucy! It is too dreadful. Tell me how it happened."

"Don't ask me, my dear!" said Dame Hartley, sadly. "Why should you hear anything so painful? It would only haunt your mind as it haunted mine for years after. The worst of it was, there was no need of it. Her mother was a young, flighty, careless girl, and she didn't look after her baby as she should have done. That is all you need know, Hilda, my dear! Poor Susan Chirk! it took the flightiness out of her, and made her the anxious, melancholy soul she has been ever since. Then Bubble was born, and soon after her husband died, and since then she has had a hard time to fend for herself. But Pink has never been any trouble to her, only a help and a comfort; and her neighbors have done what they could from time to time."

Dame Hartley might have said that she and her husband had kept this desolate widow and her children from starvation through many a long winter, and had given her the means of earning her daily bread in summer; had clothed the children, and provided comforts for the crippled girl. But this was not Nurse Lucy's way. The neighbors had done what they could, she said; and now Bubble was earning good wages for a boy, and was sure to get on well, being bright and industrious; and Mrs. Chirk took in weaving to do for the neighbors, and went out sometimes to work by the day; and so they were really getting on very well,—better than one could have hoped.

Hildegarde laid her head against the good Dame's shoulder and fell into a brown study. Nurse Lucy seemed also in a thoughtful mood; and so the two sat quietly in the soft twilight till the red glow faded in the west, and left in its stead a single star, gleaming like a living jewel in the purple sky. All the birds were asleep save the untiring whippoorwill, who presented his plea for the castigation of the unhappy William with ceaseless energy. A little night-breeze came up, and said pleasant, soft things to the leaves, which rustled gently in reply, and the crickets gave their usual evening concert, beginning with a movement in G sharp, allegro con moto. Other sound there was none, until by and by the noise of wheels was heard, and the click of old Nancy's hoofs; and out of the gathering darkness Farmer Hartley appeared, just returned from the village, whither he had gone to make arrangements about selling his hay.

"Wal, Marm Lucy," he said, cheerfully, throwing the reins on Nancy's neck and jumping from the wagon, "is that you settin' thar? 'Pears to me I see somethin' like a white apun gloomin' out o' the dark."

"Yes, Jacob," answered "Marm Lucy," "I am here, and so is Hilda. The evening has been so lovely, we have not had the heart to light the lamps, but have just been sitting here watching the sunset. We'll come in now, though," she added, leading the way into the house. "You'll be wanting some supper, my man. Or did ye stop at Cousin Sarah's?"

"I stopped at Sary's," replied the farmer. "Ho! ho! yes, Sary gave me some supper, though she warn't in no mood for seein' comp'ny, even her own kin. Poor Sary! she was in a dretful takin', sure enough!"

"Why, what was the matter?" asked Dame Hartley, as she trimmed and lighted the great lamp, and drew the short curtains of Turkey red cotton across the windows. "Is Abner sick again!"

"Shouldn't wonder if he was, by this time," replied the farmer; "but he warn't at the beginnin' of it. I'll tell ye how 'twas;" and he sat down in his great leather chair, and stretched his legs out comfortably before him, while his wife filled his pipe and brought it to him,—a little attention which she never forgot. "Sary, she bought a new bunnit yisterday!" Farmer Hartley continued, puffing away at the pipe. "She's kind o' savin', ye know, Sary is [Nurse Lucy nodded, with a knowing air], and she hadn't had a new bunnit for ten years. (I d' 'no' 's she's had one for twenty!" he added in parenthesis; "I never seed her with one to my knowledge.) Wal, the gals was pesterin' her, an' sayin' she didn't look fit to go to meetin' in the old bunnit, so 't last she giv' way, and went an' bought a new one. 'Twas one o' these newfangled shapes. What was it Lizy called it? Somethin' Chinese, I reckon. Fan Song! That was it!"

"Fanchon, wasn't it, perhaps?" asked Hilda, much amused.

"That's what I said, warn't it?" said the farmer. "Fan Song, Fan Chong,—wal, what's the odds? 'Twas a queer lookin' thing, anyhow, I sh'd think, even afore it— Wal, I'm comin' to that. Sary showed it to the gals, and they liked it fust-rate; then she laid it on the kitchen table, an' went upstairs to git some ribbons an' stuff to put on it. She rummaged round consid'able upstairs, an' when she kum down, lo and behold, the bunnit was gone! Wal, Sary hunted high, and she hunted low. She called the gals, thinkin' they'd played a trick on her, an' hidden it for fun. But they hadn't, an' they all set to an' sarched the house from garrit to cellar; but they didn't find hide nor hair o' that bunnit. At last Sary give it up, an' sot down out o' breath, an' mad enough to eat somebody. 'It's been stole!' says she. 'Some ornery critter kem along while I was upstairs,' says she, 'an' seed it lyin' thar on the table, an' kerried it off!' says she. 'I'd like to get hold of her!' says she; 'I guess she wouldn't steal no more bunnits for one while!' says she. I had come in by that time, an' she was tellin' me all about it. Jest at that minute the door opened, and Abner kem sa'nterin' in, mild and moony as usual 'Sary,' says he,—ho! ho! ho! it makes me laugh to think on't,— 'Sary,' says he, 'I wouldn't buy no more baskets without handles, ef I was you. They ain't convenient to kerry,' says he. And with that he sets down on the table—that Fan Chong bunnit! He'd been mixin' chicken feed in it, an' he'd held it fust by one side an' then by the other, an' he'd dropped it in the mud too, I reckon, from the looks of it: you never seed sech a lookin' thing in all your born days as that bunnit was. Sary, she looked at it, and then she looked at Abner, an' then at the bunnit agin; an' then she let fly."

"Poor Sarah!" said Nurse Lucy, wiping tears of merriment from her eyes. "What did she say?"

"I can't tell ye what she said," replied the farmer. "What did your old cat say when Spot caught hold of her tail the other day? An' yet there was language enough in what Sary said. I tell ye the hull dictionary was flyin' round that room for about ten minutes,—Webster's Unabridged, an' nothin' less. An' Abner, he jest stood thar, bobbin' his head up an' down, and openin' an' shettin' his mouth, as if he'd like to say somethin' if he could get a chance. But when Sary was so out of breath that she couldn't say another word, an' hed to stop for a minute, Abner jest says, 'Sary, I guess you're a little excited. Jacob an' me'll go out an' take a look at the stock,' says he, 'and come back when you're feelin' calmer.' An' he nods to me, an' out we both goes, before Sary could git her breath agin. I didn't say nothin', 'cause I was laughin' so inside 't I couldn't. Abner, he walked along kind o' solemn, shakin' his head every little while, an' openin' an' shettin' his mouth. When we got to the stable-door he looked at me a minute, and then he said, 'The tongue is a onruly member, Jacob! I thought that was kind of a curus lookin' basket, though!' and that was every word he said about it."

"Oh, what delightfully funny people!" cried Hilda. "What did the wife say when you came in to supper, Farmer Hartley?"

"She warn't thar," replied the farmer. "She had a headache, the gals said, and had gone to bed. I sh'd think she would have had a headache,—but thar," he added, rising suddenly and beginning to search in his capacious pockets, "I declar' for 't, if I hain't forgotten Huldy's letter! Sary an' her bunnit put everything else out of my head."

Hilda sprang up in delight to receive the envelope which the farmer handed to her; but her face fell a little when she saw that it was not from her parents. She reflected, however, that she had had a double letter only two days before, and that she could not expect another for a week, as Mr. and Mrs. Graham wrote always with military punctuality. There was no doubt as to the authorship of the letter. The delicate pointed handwriting, the tiny seal of gilded wax, the faint perfume which the missive exhaled, all said to her at once, "Madge Everton."

With a feeling which, if not quite reluctance, was still not quite alacrity, Hildegarde broke the pretty seal, with its Cupid holding a rose to his lips, and read as follows:—

Saratoga, July 20.

My dearest, sweetest Hilda,—Can it be possible that you have been away a whole month, and that I have not written to you? I am awfully ashamed! but I have been so too busy, it has been out of the question. Papa decided quite suddenly to come here instead of going to Long Branch; and you can imagine the frantic amount of work Mamma and I

45

had to get ready. One has to dress so much at Saratoga, you know; and we cannot just send an order to Paris, as you do, my dear Queen, for all we want, but have to scratch round (I know you don't allow your subjects to use slang, but we do scratch round, and nothing else can express it), and get things made here. I have a lovely pale blue Henrietta-cloth, made like that rose-colored gown of yours that I admire so much, and that you said I might copy. Mamma says it was awfully good of you, and that she wouldn't let any one copy her French dresses if she had them; but I told her you were awfully good, and that was why. Well, then I have a white nun's-veiling, made with triple box-plaits, and a lovely pointed overskirt, copied from a Donovan dress of Mamma's; and a dark-red surah, and oh! a perfect "frou-frou" of wash-dresses, of course; two sweet white lawns, one trimmed with valenciennes (I hate valenciennes, you know, but Mamma will make me have it, because she thinks it is jeune fille!), and one with the new Russian lace; and a pink sateen, and two or three light chambrays.

But now I know you will be dying to hear about my hats; for you always say that the hat makes the costume; and so it does! Well, my dearest, I have one Redfern hat, and only one. Mamma says I cannot expect to have more until I come out, which is bitter. However, this one is a beauty, and yet cost only thirty dollars. It goes well with nearly all my dresses, and is immensely becoming, all the girls say: very high, with long pointed wings and stiff bows. Simple, my dear, doesn't express it! You know I love simplicity; but it is Redferny to a degree, and everybody has noticed it.

Well, my dearest Queen, here am I running on about myself, as if I were not actually expiring to hear about you. What my feelings were when I called at your house on that fatal Tuesday and was told that you had gone to spend the summer on a farm in the depths of the country, passes my power to tell. I could not ask your mother many questions, for you know I am always a little bit afraid of her, though she is perfectly lovely to me! She was very quiet and sweet, as usual, and spoke as if it were the most natural thing in the world for a brilliant society girl (for that is what you are, Hilda, even though you are only a school-girl; and you never can be anything else!) to spend her summer in a wretched farm-house, among pigs and cows and dreadful ignorant people. Of course, Hilda dearest, you know that my admiration for your mother is simply immense, and that I would not for worlds say one syllable against her judgment and that of your military angel of a father; but I must say it seemed to me more than strange. I assure you I hardly closed my eyes for several nights, thinking of the misery you must be undergoing; for I know you, Hildegarde! and the thought of my proud, fastidious, high-bred Queen being condemned to associate with clowns and laborers was really more than I could bear. Do write to me, darling, and tell me how you are enduring it. You were always so sensitive; why, I can see your lip curl now, when any of the girls did anything that was not tout à fait comme il faut! and the air with which you used to say, "The little things, my dear, are the only things!" How true it is! I feel it more and more every day. So do write at once, and let me know all about your dear self. I picture you to myself sometimes, pale and thin, with the "white disdain" that some poet or other speaks of, in your face, but enduring all the horrors that you must be subjected to with your own dignity. Dearest Hilda, you are indeed a heroine!

Always, darling,
Your own deeply devoted and sympathizing
Madge.

46

Hildegarde looked up after reading this letter, and, curiously enough, her eyes fell directly on a little mirror which hung on the wall opposite. In it she saw a rosy, laughing face, which smiled back mischievously at her. There were dimples in the cheeks, and the gray eyes were fairly dancing with life and joyousness. Where was the "white disdain," the dignity, the pallor and emaciation? Could this be Madge's Queen Hildegarde? Or rather, thought the girl, with a sudden revulsion of feeling, could this Hildegarde ever have been the other? The form of "the minx," long since dissociated from her thoughts and life, seemed to rise, like Banquo's ghost, and stare at her with cold, disdainful eyes and supercilious curl of the lip. Oh dear! how dreadful it was to have been so odious! How could poor dear Papa and Mamma, bless them, have endured her as they did, so patiently and sweetly? But they should see when they came back! She had only just begun yet; but there were two months still before her, and in that time what could she not do? They should be surprised, those dear parents! And Madge—why, Madge would be surprised too. Poor Madge! To think of her in Saratoga, prinking and preening herself like a gay bird, in the midst of a whirl of dress and diamonds and gayety, with no fields, no woods, no glen, no—no kitchen! Hilda looked about the room which she had learned so to love, trying to fancy Madge Everton in it; remembering, too, the bitterness of her first feeling about it. The lamplight shone cheerily on the yellow painted walls, the shining floor, the gleaming brass, copper, and china. It lighted up the red curtains and made a halo round good Nurse Lucy's head as she bent over her sewing; it played on the farmer's silver-bowed spectacles as he pored with knitted brows and earnest look over the weekly paper which he had brought from the village. The good, kind farmer! Hilda gazed at him as he sat all unconscious, and wondered why she had not seen at once how handsome he really was. The broad forehead, with its deep, thoughtful furrows; the keen, yet kindly blue eyes; the "sable-silvered" hair and beard, which, if not exactly smooth, were still so picturesque, so leonine; the firm, perhaps obstinate, mouth, which could speak so wisely and smile so cordially,—all these combined to make up what the newspapers would call a "singularly attractive exterior." And "Oh! how good he has been to me!" thought Hilda. "I believe he is the best man in the world, next to papa." Then she thought of Madge again, and tried to fancy her in her Redfern hat,—pretty Madge, with her black eyes and curly fringe, under the "simplicity" of the heaven-aspiring wings and bows; and as she smiled at the image, there rose beside it the fair head of Pink Chirk, looking out like a white rose from the depths of her dingy straw tunnel. Then she fancied herself saying airily (she knew just how she used to say it), "The little things, my dear, are the only things!" and then she laughed aloud at the very funniness of it.

"Hut! tut!" said Farmer Hartley, looking up from his paper with a smile. "What's all this? Are ye keepin' all the jokes to yerself, Huldy?"

"It is only my letter that is so funny," replied Hilda. "I don't believe it would seem so funny to you, Farmer Hartley, because you don't know the writer. But have you finished your paper, and are you ready for Robin Hood?"

"Wal, I am, Huldy!" said the good farmer, laying aside his paper and rubbing his hands with an air of pleasurable anticipation. "'Pears to me we left that good-lookin' singin' chap—what was his name?"

"Allan-a-Dale!" said Hilda, smiling.

47

"Ah!" said the farmer; "Allan-a-Dale. 'Pears to me we left him in rayther a ticklish situation."

"Oh, but it comes out all right!" cried Hilda, joyously, rising to fetch the good brown book which she loved. "You will see in the next chapter how delightfully Robin gets him out of the difficulty." She ran and brought the book and drew her chair up to the table, and all three prepared for an hour of solid enjoyment. "But before I begin," she said, "I want you to promise, Farmer Hartley, to take me with you the next time you go to the village. I must buy a hat for Pink Chirk."

CHAPTER IX.

THE OLD CAPTAIN.

"Let—me—see!" said Farmer Hartley, as he gathered up the reins and turned old Nancy's head towards the village, while Hildegarde, on the seat beside him, turned back to wave a merry farewell to Nurse Lucy, who stood smiling in the porch. "Let—me—see! Hev you ben off the farm before, Huldy, sence you kem here?"

"Not once!" replied Hilda, cheerily. "And I don't believe I should be going now, Farmer Hartley, if it were not for Pink's hat. I promised myself that she should not wear that ugly straw sun-bonnet again. I wonder why anything so hideous was ever invented."

"A straw bunnit, do ye mean?" said the farmer; "somethin' like a long sugar-scoop, or a tunnel like?"

"Yes, just that!" said Hilda; "and coming down over her poor dear eyes so that she cannot see anything, except for a few inches straight before her."

"Wal!" said the farmer, meditatively, "I remember when them bunnits was considered reel hahnsome. Marm Lucy had one when she was a gal; I mind it right well. A white straw it was, with blue ribbons on top of it. It come close round her pooty face, an' I used to hev to sidle along and get round in front of her before I could get a look at her. I hed rayther a grudge agin the bunnit on that account; but I supposed it was hahnsome, as everybody said so. I never see a bunnit o' that kind," he continued, "without thinkin' o' Mis' Meeker an' 'Melia Tyson. I swan! it makes me laugh now to think of 'em."

"Who were they?" asked Hildegarde, eagerly, for she delighted in the farmer's stories. "Please tell me about them!"

The farmer shook his head, as was his wont when he was about to relapse into reminiscences, and gave old Nancy several thoughtful taps with the whip, which she highly resented.

"Ol' Mis' Meeker," he said, presently, "she was a character, she was! She didn't belong hereabouts, but down South somewhere, but she was cousin to Cephas Tyson, an' when Cephas' wife died, she came to stop with him a spell, an' look out for his children. Three children there was, little Cephas, an' Myrick, an' 'Melia. 'Melia, she was a peart, lively little gal, with snappin' black eyes, an' consid'ble of a will of her own; an' Mis'

Meeker, she was pooty stout, an' she took things easy, jest as they kem, an' let the children—an' 'Melia specially—do pooty much as they'd a mind to. Wal, one day I happened in to see Cephas about a pair o' steers I was thinkin' o' buyin'. Cephas was out; but Mis' Meeker said he'd be right in, she reckoned, an' asked me to take a cheer an' wait. So I sot down, an' while I was waitin', in come 'Melia, an' says she, 'Say, Aunt Cilly (Mis' Meeker's name was Priscilla)—Say, Aunt Cilly, can I go down an' play with Eddie? He wants me to come, reel bad. Can I, Aunt Cilly?' 'Not to-day, dearie,' says Mis' Meeker; 'you was down to play with Eddie yesterday, an' I reckon that'll do for one while!' she says. I looked at little 'Melia, an' her eyes was snappin' like coals. She didn't say nothin', but she jest took an' shoved her elbow right through the plate-glass winder. Ho! ho! Cephas had had his house made over, an' he was real proud of his plate-glass winders. I d' 'no' how much they'd cost him, but 'twas a pooty good sum. An' she shoved her elbow right through it and smashed it into shivers. I jumped up, kind o' startled by the crash. But ol' Mis' Meeker, she jes' looked up, as if she was a leetle bit surprised, but nothin' wuth mentionin'. 'Why, honey!' says she, in her slow, drawlin' kind o' way, 'I didn't know ye wanted to go that bad! Put on yer bunnit, an' go an' play with Eddie this minute!' says she. Ho! ho! ho! Them was her very words. An' 'Melia, she tossed her bunnit on (one o' them straw Shakers it was, an' that's what made me think o' the story), and jes' shook the glass out'n her sleeve,—I d' 'no' why the child warn't cut to pieces, but she didn't seem t' have got no hurt,—and made a face at her aunt, an' off she went. That's the way them children was brought up."

"Poor things!" cried Hilda. "What became of them, Farmer Hartley?"

"'Melia, she run off an' married a circus feller," replied the farmer, "an' the boys, I don't rightly know what become of 'em. They went out West, I b'lieve; an' after 'Melia married, Cephas went out to jine 'em, an' I ain't heerd nothin' of 'em for years."

By this time they were rattling through the main street of the little village, and presently stopped before an unpretending little shop, in the window of which were displayed some rather forlorn-looking hats and bonnets.

"Here y'are, Huldy!" said the farmer, pointing to the shop with a flourish of his whip. "Here's whar ye git the styles fust hand. Hev to come from New York to Glenfield to git the reel thing, ye see."

"I see!" laughed Hilda, springing lightly from the wagon.

"I'll call for ye in 'bout half an hour;" and with a kindly nod the farmer drove away down the street.

Hildegarde entered the dingy little shop with some misgivings, "I hope I shall find something fresh!" she said to herself; "those things in the window look as if they had been there since the Flood." She quickly made friends with the brisk little milliner, and they were soon turning over the meagre store of hats, trimmed and untrimmed.

"This is real tasty!" said the little woman, lifting with honest pride an alarming structure of green satin, which some straggling cock's feathers were doing their best to hide.

Hilda shuddered, but said pleasantly, "Rather heavy for summer; don't you think so? It would be better for a winter hat. What is this?" she added, drawing from the farthest recesses of the box an untrimmed hat of rough yellow straw. "I think perhaps this will do, Miss Bean."

"Oh my land, no! you don't want that!" cried the little milliner, aghast. "That's only common doin's, anyhow; and it's been in that box three years. Them shapes ain't worn now."

"Never mind!" said Hilda, merrily; "it is perfectly fresh, and I like the shape. Just wait till you see it trimmed, Miss Bean. May I rummage a little among your drawers? I will not toss the things about."

A piece of dotted mull and a bunch of soft pink roses rewarded her search; and with these and a bit of rose-colored ribbon she proceeded to make the rough straw into so dainty and bewitching a thing that Miss Bean sat fairly petrified with amazement on her little hair-cloth sofa in the back shop. "Why! why!" she said. "If that ain't the beat of all! It's the tastiest hat I ever see. You never told me you'd learned the trade!"

This last was rather reproachfully said; and Hilda, much amused, hastened to reassure the good woman.

"Indeed, I never learned the trade," she said. "I take to it naturally, I think; and I have watched my mother, who does it much better than I."

"She must be a first-class trimmer, then!" replied Miss Bean, emphatically. "Works in one o' them big houses in New York, I reckon, don't she?"

Hildegarde laughed; but before she could reply, Miss Bean went on to say: "Wal, you're a stranger to me, but you've got a pooty good count'nance, an' ye kem with Farmer Hartley; that's reference enough." She paused and reflected, while Hildegarde, putting the finishing touches to the pretty hat, wondered what was coming. "I wasn't calc'latin' to hire help this summer," continued the milliner; "but you're so handy, and yer ma could give ye idees from time to time. So if ye'd like a job, I d' 'no' but I'd like to hire ye."

The heiress of all the Grahams wanted to laugh at this naïve proposal, but good feeling and good manners alike forbade. She thanked Miss Bean for her kind offer, and explained that she was only spending her school vacation at Hartley Farm; that her time was fully occupied, etc., etc.

The little milliner looked so disappointed that Hilda was seized with a royal impulse, and offered to "go over" the hats in the window while she waited for Farmer Hartley, and freshen them up a bit.

"Well, I wish't ye would!" said poor Miss Bean. "Fact is, I ain't done so well as I c'd wish this season. Folks is dretful 'fraid o' buyin' new things nowadays."

Then followed a series of small confidences on the hair-cloth sofa, while Hilda's fingers flew about the forlorn hats and bonnets, changing a ribbon here and a flower there, patting and poking, and producing really marvellous results. Another tale of patient labor, suffering, privation. An invalid mother and an "innocent" brother for this frail little woman to support. Doctors' bills and hard times, and stingy patrons who were "as 'fraid of a dollar-bill as if 'twas the small-pox." Hilda's eyes filled with tears of sympathy, and one great drop fell on the green satin hat, but was instantly covered by the wreath of ivy which was replacing the staring cock's feathers.

"Wal, I declare to gracious!" exclaimed Miss Bean. "You'd never know that for the same hat, now, would ye? I thought 'twas han'some before, but it's enough site han'somer now. I shouldn' wonder a mite if Mis' Peasley bought that hat now. She's been kind o' hankerin' arter it, the last two or three times she was in here; but every time she tried it on, she'd say No, 'twas too showy, she guessed. Wal, I do say, you make a gret mistake not goin' into the trade, for you're born to it, that's plain. When a pusson's born to a thing, he's thrown away, you may say, on anything else. What was you thinkin'—"

But at this moment came a cheery call of "Huldy! Huldy!" and Hildegarde, cutting short the little woman's profuse thanks and invitations to call again, bade her a cordial good-by, and ran out to the wagon, carrying her purchase neatly done up in brown paper.

"Stiddy thar!" said the farmer, making room for her on the seat beside him. "Look out for the ile-can, Huldy! Bought out the hull shop, hev ye? Wal, I sh'll look for gret things the next few days. Huddup thar, Nancy!" And they went jingling back along the street again.

As they passed the queer little shops, with their antiquated signboards, the farmer had something to say about each one. How Omnium Grabb here, the grocer, missed his dried apples one morning, and how he accused his chore-boy, who was his sister's son too, of having eaten them,—"As if any livin' boy would pick out dried apples to eat, when he hed a hull store to choose from!" and how the very next day a man coming to buy a pair of boots, Omnium Grabb hooked down a pair from the ceiling, where all the boots hung, and found them "chock full" of dried apples, which the rats had been busily storing in them and their companion pairs.

How Enoch Pillsbury, the "'pottecary, like t' ha' killed" Old Man Grout, sending him writing fluid instead of the dark mixture for his "dyspepsy."

How Beulah Perkins, who lived over the dry-goods store, had been bedridden for nineteen years, till the house where she was living caught fire, "whereupon she jumped out o' bed an' grabbed an umbrella an' opened it, an' ran down street in her red-flannel gownd, with the umbrella over her head, shoutin', 'Somebody go save my bedstid! I ain't stirred from it for nineteen years, an' I ain't never goin' to stir from it agin. Somebody go save my bedstid!'"

"And was it saved?" asked Hilda, laughing.

51

"No," said the farmer; "'t wa'n't wuth savin', nohow. Besides, if't hed been, she'd ha' gone back to it an' stayed there. Hosy Grout, who did her chores, kicked it into the fire; an' she was a well woman to the day of her death."

Now the houses straggled farther and farther apart, and at last the village was fairly left behind. Old Nancy pricked up her ears and quickened her pace a little, looking right and left with glances of pleasure as the familiar fields ranged themselves along either side of the road. Hilda too was glad to be in the free country again, and she looked with delight at the banks of fern, the stone walls covered with white starry clematis, and the tangle of blackberry vines which made the pleasant road so fragrant and sweet. She was silent for some time. At last she said, half timidly, "Farmer Hartley, you promised to tell me more about your father some day. Don't you think this would be a good time? I have been so much interested by what I have heard of him."

"That's curus, now," said Farmer Hartley slowly, flicking the dust with the long lash of his whip. "It's curus, Huldy, that you sh'd mention Father jest now, 'cause I happened to be thinkin' of him myself that very minute. Old Father," he added meditatively, "wal, surely, he was a character, Father was. Folks about here," he said, turning suddenly to Hilda and looking keenly at her, "think Father was ravin' crazy, or mighty nigh it. But he warn't nothin' o' the sort. His mind was as keen as a razor, an' as straight-edged, 'xcept jest on one subject. On that he was, so to say, a little—wal—a little tetched."

"And that was—?" queried Hilda.

"Why, ye see, Huldy, Father had been a sea-farin' man all his days, an' he'd seen all manner o' countries an' all manner o' folks; and 'tain't to be wondered at ef he got a leetle bit confoosed sometimes between the things he'd seen and the things he owned. Long'n short of it was, Father thought he hed a kind o' treasure hid away somewhar, like them pirate fellers used to hev. Ef they did hev it!" he added slowly. "I never more'n half believed none o' them yarns; but Father, he thought he hed it, an' no mistake. 'D'ye think I was five years coastin' round Brazil for nothin'?' he says. 'There's di'monds in Brazil,' he says, 'whole mines of 'em; an' there's some di'monds out o' Brazil too;' and then he'd wink, and laugh out hearty, the way he used. He was always laughin', Father was. An' when times was hard, he'd say to my mother, 'Wealthy, we won't sell the di'monds yet a while. Not this time, Wealthy; but they're thar, you know, my woman, they're thar!' And when my mother'd say, 'Whar to goodness be they, Thomas?' he'd only chuckle an' laugh an' shake his head. Then thar was his story about the ruby necklace. How we youngsters used to open our eyes at that! Believed it too, every word of it."

"Oh! what was it?" cried Hilda. "Tell me, and I will believe it too!"

"He used to tell of a Malay pirate," said the farmer, "that he fit and licked somewhere off in the South Seas,—when he sailed the 'Lively Polly,' that was. She was a clipper, Father always said; an' he run aboard the black fellers, and smashed their schooner, an' throwed their guns overboard, an' demoralized 'em ginerally. They took to their boats an' paddled off, what was left of 'em, an' he an' his crew sarched the schooner, an' found a woman locked up in the cabin,—an Injin princess, father said she was,—an' they holdin' her for ransom. Wal, Father found out somehow whar she come from,— Javy, or Mochy, or some o' them places out o' the spice-box,—an' he took her home, an'

52

hunted up her parents an' guardeens, an' handed her over safe an' sound. They—the guardeens—was gret people whar they lived, an' they wanted to give Father a pot o' money; but he said he warn't that kind. 'I'm a Yankee skipper!' says he. "Twas as good as a meal o' vittles to me to smash that black feller!' says he. 'I don't want no pay for it. An' as for the lady, 'twas a pleasure to obleege her,' he says; 'an' I'd do it agin any day in the week, 'xcept Sunday, when I don't fight, ez a rewl, when I kin help it.' Then the princess, she tried to kiss his hand; but Father said he guessed that warn't quite proper, an' the guardeens seemed to think so too. So then she took a ruby necklace off her neck (she was all done up in shawls, Father said, an' silk, an' gold chains, an' fur an' things, so 's 't he couldn' see nothin' but her eyes; but they was better wuth seein' than any other woman's hull face that ever he see), and gave it to him, an' made signs that he must keep that, anyhow. Then she said somethin' to one o' the guardeens who spoke a little Portuguese, Father understandin' it a little too, and he told Father she said these was the drops of her blood he had saved, an' he must keep it to remember her. Jest like drops of blood, he said the rubies was, strung along on a gold chain. So he took it, an' said he warn't likely to forget about it; an' then he made his bow, an' the guardeens said he was their father, an' their mother, an' their great-aunt, an' I d' 'no' what all, an' made him stay to supper, an' he didn't eat nothin' for a week arterward."

The farmer paused, and Hildegarde drew a long breath, "Oh!" she cried, "what a delightful story, Farmer Hartley! And you don't believe it? I do, every word of it! I am sure it is true!"

"Wal, ye see," said the farmer, meditatively; "Ef' t was true, what become o' the necklace? That's what I say. Father believed it, sure enough, and he thought he hed that necklace, as sure as you think you hev that bunnit in yer hand. But 'twarn't never found, hide nor hair of it."

"Might he not have sold it?" Hilda suggested.

Farmer Hartley shook his head, "No," he said, "he warn't that kind. Besides, he thought to the day of his death that he hed it, sure enough. 'Thar's the princess's necklace!' he'd say; 'don't ye forgit that, Wealthy! Along with the di'monds, ye know.' And then he'd laugh like he was fit to bust. Why, when he was act'lly dyin', so fur gone 't he couldn' speak plain, he called me to him, an' made signs he wanted to tell me somethin'. I stooped down clost, an' he whispered somethin'; but all I could hear was 'di'monds,' and 'dig,' and then in a minute 'twas all over. Poor old Father! He'd been a good skipper, an' a good man all his days."

He was silent for a time, while Hilda pondered over the story, which she could not make up her mind to disbelieve altogether.

"Wal! wal! and here we are at the old farm agin!" said the farmer presently, as old Nancy turned in at the yellow gate. "Here I've been talkin' the everlastin' way home, ain't I? You must herry and git into the house, Huldy, for I d' 'no' how the machine's managed to run without ye all this time. I sha'n't take ye out agin ef I find anythin's wrong."

CHAPTER X.

53

A PARTY OF PLEASURE.

On a certain lovely afternoon the three happiest people in the world (so they styled themselves, and they ought to know) were gathered together in a certain spot, which was next to the prettiest spot in the world.

"You should have had the prettiest, Pink," said Hilda, "but we could not get your chair down into the glen, you know. My poor, dear Pink, you have never seen the glen, have you?"

"No," answered Pink Chirk, cheerily. "But I have heard so much about it, I really feel as if I had seen it, almost. And indeed I don't think it can be much lovelier than this place."

However that might be, the place they had chosen was certainly pretty enough to satisfy any one. Not far from Mrs. Chirk's cottage was a little pine-grove, easy of access, and with trees far enough apart to allow the wheeled chair to pass between them. And in the grove, just in a little open space where two or three trees had been cut away, was a great black rock, with ferns growing in all its cracks and crannies, and a tiny birch-tree waving like a green and white plume on its top. And at the foot of the rock—oh, what a wonderful thing!—a slender thread of crystal water came trickling out, as cold as ice and as clear as—as itself; for nothing else could be so clear. Bubble had made a little wooden trough to hold this fairy stream, and it gurgled along the trough and tumbled over the end of it with as much agitation and consequence as if it were the Niagara River in person. And under the rock and beside the stream was a bank of moss and ferns most lovely to behold, most luxurious to sit upon. On this bank sat Queen Hildegarde, with Bubble at her feet as usual; and beside her, in her chair, sat sweet Pink, looking more like a white rose than ever, with her fresh white dimity gown and her pretty hat. Hilda was very busy over a mysterious-looking basket, from whose depths she now drew a large napkin, which she spread on the smooth green moss. A plate of sandwiches came next, and some cold chicken, and six of Dame Hartley's wonderful apple-turnovers.

"Now, Bubble," said Hilda, "where are those birch-bark cups that you made for us? I have brought nothing to drink out of."

"I'll fetch 'em, Miss Hildy," cried Bubble, springing up with alacrity. "I clean forgot 'em. Say, Pink, shall I—? would you?" and he made sundry enigmatical signs to his sister.

"Yes, certainly," said Pink; "of course."

The boy ran off, and Hilda fell to twisting pine tassels together into a kind of fantastic garland, while Pink looked on with beaming eyes.

"Pink," said Hilda, presently, "how is it that you speak so differently from Bubble and your mother,—so much better English, I mean? Have you—but no; you told me you never went to school."

54

"It was Faith," said Pink, with a look of tender sadness,—"Faith Hartley. She wanted to be a teacher, and we studied together always. Dear Faith! I wish you had known her, Miss Graham."

"You promised not to call me Miss Graham again, Pink," said Hildegarde, reproachfully. "It is absurd, and I won't have it."

"Well, Hilda, then," said Pink, shyly. "I wish you had known Faith, Hilda; you would have loved her very much, I know."

"I am sure I should," said Hilda, warmly. "Tell me more about her. Why did she want to teach when she was so happy at home?"

"She loved children very much," said Pink, "and liked to be with them. She thought that if she studied hard, she could teach them more than the district school teachers about here generally do, and in a better way. I think she would have done a great deal of good," she added, softly.

"Oh! why did she die?" cried Hilda. "She was so much needed! It broke her father's heart, and her mother's, and almost yours, my Pink. Why was it right for her to die?"

"It was right, dear," said Pink, gently; "that is all we can know. 'Why' isn't answered in this world. My granny used to say,—

"'Never lie!
Never pry!
Never ask the reason why!'"
Hilda shook her head, and was about to reply earnestly; but at this moment Bubble came bounding back with something in his arms,—something covered with an old shawl; something alive, which did not like the shawl, and which struggled, and made plaintive little noises, which the boy tried vainly to repress.

"Say, Miss Hildy," he cried, eagerly, "do ye like—be still, ye critter; hesh, I tell ye!— do you like purps?"

"'SAY, MISS HILDY,—DO YOU LIKE PURPS?'"
"'SAY, MISS HILDY,—DO YOU LIKE PURPS?'"
"'Purps,' Bubble?" repeated Hilda, wonderingly. "What are they? And what have you there,—your poor old cat? Let her go! For shame, you naughty boy!"

"Puppies, he means," whispered Pink.

"'Cause if ye do," cried the breathless Bubble, still struggling with his shrouded captive, "I've got one here as—Wal, thar! go 'long, ye pesky critter, if ye will!" for the poor puppy had made one frantic effort, and leaped from his arms to the ground, where it rolled over and over, a red and green plaid mass, with a white tail sticking out of one end. On being unrolled, it proved to be a little snow-white, curly creature, with long ears and large, liquid eyes, whose pathetic glance went straight to Hilda's heart.

"Oh, the little darling!" she cried, taking him up in her arms; "the pretty, pretty creature! Is he really for me, Bubble? Thank you very much. I shall love him dearly, I know."

"I'm glad ye like him," said Bubble, looking highly gratified. "Hosy Grout giv him an' another one to me yes'day, over 't the village. He was goin' to drownd 'em, an' I wouldn' let him, an' he said I might hev 'em ef I wanted 'em. I knew Pink would like to hev one, an' I thought mebbe you liked critters, an' so—"

"Good Bubble!" said Hilda, stroking the little dog's curly head. "And what shall I call him, Pink? Let us each think of a name, and then choose the best."

There was a pause, and then Bubble said, "Call him Scott, after the bold Buckle-oh!"

"Or Will, for 'the wily Belted Will,'" said Pink, who was as inveterate a ballad-lover as her brother.

"I think Jock is a good name," said Hildegarde,—"Jock o' Hazeldean, you know. I think I will call him Jock." The others assented, and the puppy was solemnly informed of the fact, and received a chicken-bone in honor of the occasion. Then the three friends ate their dinner, and very merry they were over it. Hildegarde crowned Pink with the pine-tassel wreath, and declared that she looked like a priestess of Diana.

"No, she don't," said Bubble, looking up from his cold chicken; "she looks like Lars Porsena of Clusium sot in his ivory cheer, on'y she ain't f'erce enough. Hold up yer head, Pinky, an' look real savage, an' I'll do Horatius at the Bridge."

Pink did her best to look savage, and Zerubbabel stood up and delivered "Horatius" with much energy and appropriate action, to the great amusement of his audience. A stout stick, cut from a neighboring thicket, served for the "good Roman steel;" and with this he cut and slashed and stabbed with furious energy, reciting the lines meanwhile with breathless ferocity. He slew the "great Lord of Luna," and on the imaginary body he—

"Right firmly pressed his heel,
And thrice and four times tugged amain,
Ere he wrenched out the steel."
But when he cried—

"What noble Lucumo comes next
To taste our Roman cheer?"
the puppy, who had been watching the scene with kindling eyes, and ears and tail of eager inquiry, could bear it no longer, but flung himself valiantly into the breach, and barked defiance, dancing about in front of Horatius and snapping furiously at his legs. Alas, poor puppy! He was hailed as "Sextus," and bade "welcome" by the bold Roman, who forthwith charged upon him, and drove him round and round the grove till he sought safety and protection in the lap of Lars Porsena herself. Then the bridge came down, and Horatius, climbing nimbly to the top of the rock, apostrophized his Father Tiber, sheathed his good sword by his side (i.e., rammed his stick into and through his

breeches pocket), and with his jacket on his back plunged headlong in the tide, and swam valiantly across the pine-strewn surface of the little glade.

Bubble's performance was much applauded by the two girls, who, in the characters of Lars Porsena and Mamilius, "Prince of the Latian name," had surveyed the whole with dignified amazement. And when the boy, exhausted with his heroic exertions, threw himself down on the pine-needles and begged "Miss Hildy" to sing to them, she readily consented, and sang "Jock o' Hazeldean" and "Come o'er the stream, Charlie!" so sweetly that the little fat birds sat still on the branches to listen. A faint glow stole into Pink's wan cheek, and her blue eyes sparkled with pleasure; while Bubble bobbed his head, and testified his delight by drumming with his heels on the ground and begging for more. "A ballid now, Miss Hildy, please," he cried.

"Well," said Hildegarde, nothing loth, "what shall it be?"

"One with some fightin' in it," replied Bubble, promptly.

So Hildegarde began:—

"Down Deeside cam Inverey,
Whistling and playing;
He's lighted at Brackley gates
At the day's dawing."
And went on to tell of the murder of "bonnie Brackley" and of the treachery of his young wife:—

"There's grief in the kitchen,
And mirth in the ha';
But the Baron o' Brackley
Is dead and awa'."
So the ballad ended, leaving Bubble full of sanguinary desires anent the descendants of the false Inverey. "I—I—I'd like jest to git holt o' some o' them fellers!" he exclaimed. "They wouldn't go slaughterin' round no gret amount when I'd finished with em', I tell ye!" And he flourished his stick, and looked so fierce that the puppy yelped piteously, expecting another onslaught.

"And now, Pink," said Hilda, "we have just time for a story before we go home. Bubble has told me about your stories, and I want very much to hear one."

"Oh, Hilda, they are not worth telling twice!" protested Pink; "I just make them for Bubble when he takes me out on Sunday. It's all I can do for the dear lad."

"Don't you mind her, Miss Hildy," said Bubble; "they're fustrate stories, an' she tells 'em jest like p—'rithmetic. Go ahead, Pink! Tell the one about the princess what looked in the glass all the time."

So Pink, in her low, sweet voice, told the story of

The Vain Princess.

Once upon a time there lived a princess who was so beautiful that it was a wonder to look at her. But she was also very vain; and her beauty was of no use or pleasure to anybody, for she sat and looked in her mirror all day long, and never thought of doing anything else.

The mirror was framed in beaten gold, but the gold was not so bright as her shining locks; and all about its rim great sapphires were set, but they were dim and gray, compared with the blue of her lovely eyes. So there she sat all day in a velvet chair, clad in a satin gown with fringes of silver and pearl; and nobody in the world was one bit the better for her or her beauty.

Now, one day the princess looked at herself so long and so earnestly that she fell fast asleep in her velvet chair, with the golden mirror in her lap. While she slept, a gust of wind blew the casement window open, and a rose that was growing on the wall outside peeped in. It was a poor little feeble white rose, which had climbed up the wall in a straggling fashion, and had no particular strength or beauty or sweetness. Every one who saw it from the outside said, "What a wretched little plant! Why is it not cut down?" and the rose trembled when it heard this, for it was as fond of life as if it were beautiful, and it still hoped for better days. Inside, no one thought about it at all; for the beautiful princess never left her chair to open the window.

Now, when the rose saw the princess it was greatly delighted, for it had often heard of her marvellous beauty. It crept nearer and nearer, and gazed at the golden wonder of her hair, her ivory skin under which the blushes came and went as she slept, and her smiling lips. "Ah!" sighed the rose, "if I had only a tinge of that lovely red, I should be finer than all the other roses." And as it gazed, the thought came into its mind: "Why should I not steal a little of this wondrous beauty? Here it is of no use to anybody. If I had it, I would delight every one who passed by with my freshness and sweetness, and people would be the better for seeing a thing so lovely."

So the rose crept to the princess's feet, and climbed up over her satin gown, and twined about her neck and arms, and about her lovely golden head. And it stole the blush from her cheek, and the crimson from her lips, and the gold from her hair. And the princess grew pale and paler; but the rose blushed red and redder, and its golden heart made the room bright, and its sweetness filled the air. It grew and grew, and now new buds and leaves and blossoms appeared; and when at last it left the velvet chair and climbed out of the casement again, it was a glorious plant, such as had never before been seen. All the passers-by stopped to look at it and admire it. Little children reached up to pluck the glowing blossoms, and sick and weary people gained strength and courage from breathing their delicious perfume. The world was better and happier for the rose, and the rose knew it, and was glad.

But when the princess awoke, she took up her golden mirror again, and looking in it, saw a pale and wrinkled and gray-haired woman looking at her. Then she shrieked, and flung the mirror on the ground, and rushed out of her palace into the wide world. And wherever she went she cried, "I am the beautiful princess! Look at me and see my beauty; for I will show it to you now!" But nobody looked at her, for she was withered and ugly; and nobody cared for her, because she was selfish and vain. So she made no more difference in the world than she had made before. But the rose is blossoming still, and fills the air with its sweetness.

"My Pink," said Hildegarde, tenderly, as she walked beside her friend's chair on their homeward way, "you are shut up like the princess; but instead of the rose stealing your sweetness, you have stolen the sweetness of all the roses, and taken it into your prison with you."

"I 'shut up,' Hilda?" cried Pink, opening wide eyes of wonder and reproach. "Do you call this being shut up? See what I have had to-day! Enough pleasure to think about for a year. And even without it,—even before you came, Hilda,—why, I am the happiest girl in the world, and I ought to be."

Hildegarde stooped and kissed the pale forehead. "Yes, dear, I think you are," she said; "but I should like you to have all the pleasant and bright and lovely things in the world, my Pink."

"Well, I have the best of them," said Pink Chirk, smiling brightly,—"home and love, and friends and flowers. And as for the rest, why, dear Hilda, what is the use in thinking about things one has not?"

After this, which was part of Pink's little code of philosophy, she fell a-musing happily, while Hilda walked beside her in a kind of silent rage, almost hating herself for the fulness of vigor, the superabundant health and buoyancy, which she felt in every limb. She looked sidelong at the transparent cheek, the wasted frame, the unearthly radiance of the blue eyes. This girl was just her own age, and had never walked! It could not, it must not, be so always. Thoughts thronged into her mind of the great New York physicians and the wonders they had wrought. Might it not be possible? Could not something be done? The blood coursed more quickly through her veins, and she laid her hand on that of the crippled girl with a sudden impulse of protection and tenderness.

Pink Chirk looked up with a wondering smile. "Why, Hildegarde," she said, "you look like the British warrior queen you told me about yesterday. I was just thinking what a comfort it is to live now, instead of in those dreadful murdering times that the ballads tell of."

"I druther ha' lived then!" cried Bubble, from behind the chair. "If I hed, I'd ha' got hold o' that Inverey feller."

CHAPTER XI.

THE WARRIOR QUEEN.

Happily, happily, the days and weeks slipped by at Hartley Farm; and now September was half gone, and in two weeks more Hilda's parents would return. The letter had just arrived which fixed the date of their homecoming and Hildegarde had carried it upstairs to feast on it in her own room. She sat by the window in the little white rocking-chair, and read the words over and over again. In two weeks—really in two little weeks—she should see her mother again! It was too good to be true.

"Dragons, do you hear?" she cried, turning towards the wash-handstand. "You have seen my mother, Dragons, and she has washed her little blessed face in your bowl. I should think that might have stopped your ramping, if anything could. Or have you been waving your paws for joy ever since? I may have been unjust to you, Dragons."

The blue dragons, as usual, refused to commit themselves; and, as usual, the gilt cherubs round the looking-glass were shocked at their rudeness, and tried to atone for it by smiling as hard as they possibly could.

"Such dear, sympathetic cherubs!" said the happy girl, bending forward to kiss one of them as she was brushing her hair. "You do not ramp and glower when one tells you that one's mother is coming home. I know you are glad, you dear old things!"

And then, suddenly, even while she was laughing at the cherubs, a thought struck her which sent a pang through her heart. The cherubs would still smile, just the same, when she was gone! Ah! it was not all delight, this great news. There was sorrow mingled with the rapture. Her heart was with her parents, of course. The mere thought of seeing her mother's face, of hearing her father's voice, sent the blood dancing through her veins. And yet—she must leave the farm; she must leave Nurse Lucy and the farmer, and they would miss her. They loved her; ah! how could they help it, when she loved them so much? And the pain came again at her heart as she recalled the sad smile with which the farmer had handed her this letter. "Good news for you, Huldy," he said, "but bad for the rest of us, I reckon!" Had he had word also, or did he just know that this was about the time they had meant to return? Oh, but she would come out so often to the farm! Papa and mamma would be willing, would wish her to come; and she could not live long at a time in town, without refreshing herself with a breath of real air, country air. She might have wilted along somehow for sixteen years; but she had never been really alive—had she?—till this summer.

Pink and Bubble too! they would miss her almost as much. But that did not trouble her, for she had a plan in her head for Pink and Bubble,—a great plan, which was to be whispered to Papa almost the very moment she saw him,—not quite the very moment, but the next thing to it. The plan would please Nurse Lucy and the farmer too,—would please them almost as much as it delighted her to think about it.

Happy thought! She would go down now and tell the farmer about it. Nurse Lucy was lying down with a bad headache, she knew; but the farmer was still in the kitchen. She heard him moving about now, though he had said he was going off to the orchard. She would steal in softly and startle him, and then—

Full of happy and loving thoughts, Hildegarde slipped quietly down the stairs and across the hall, and peeped in at the kitchen-door to see what the farmer was doing. He was at the farther end of the room, with his back turned to her, stooping down over his desk. What was he doing? What a singular attitude he was in! Then, all in a moment, Hilda's heart seemed to stop beating, and her breath came thick and short; for she saw that this man before her was not the farmer. The farmer had not long elf-locks of black hair straggling over his coat-collar; he was not round-shouldered or bow-legged; above all, he would not be picking the lock of his own desk, for this was what the man before her was doing. Silent as her own shadow, Hildegarde slipped back into the hall and stood still a moment, collecting her thoughts. What should she do? Call Dame Hartley? The "poor dear" was suffering much, and why should she be disturbed? Run to find the farmer? She might have to run all over the farm! No; she would attend to this herself. She was not in the least afraid. She knew pretty well what ugly face would look up at her when she spoke; for she felt sure that the slouching, ungainly figure was that of Simon Hartley. Her heart burned with indignation against the graceless, thankless churl who could rob the man on whose charity he had been living for two years. She made a step forward, with words of righteous wrath on her lips; then paused, as a new thought struck her. This man was an absolute ruffian; and though she believed him to be an absolute coward also, still he must know that she and Dame Hartley were alone in the house. He must know also that the farmer was at some distance, else he would not have ventured to do this. What should she do? she asked herself again. She looked round her, and her eyes fell upon the old horse-pistol which rested on a couple of hooks over the door. The farmer had taken it down only a day or two before, to show it to her and tell her its story. It was not loaded, but Simon did not know that. She stepped lightly up on a chair, and in a moment had taken the pistol down. It was a formidable-looking weapon, and Hildegarde surveyed it with much satisfaction as she turned once more to enter the kitchen. Unloaded as it was, it gave her a feeling of entire confidence; and her voice was quiet and steady as she said:

"Simon Hartley, what are you doing to your uncle's desk?"

The man started violently and turned round, his hands full of papers, which he had taken from one of the drawers. He changed color when he saw "the city gal," as he invariably termed Hilda, and he answered sullenly, "Gitt'n someth'n for Uncle."

"That is not true," said Hildegarde, quietly, "I have heard your uncle expressly forbid you to go near that desk. Put those papers back!"

The man hesitated, his little, ferret eyes shifting uneasily from her to the desk and back again. "I guess I ain't goin' to take orders from no gal!" he muttered, huskily.

"Put those papers back!" repeated Hildegarde sternly, with a sudden light in her gray eyes which made the rascal step backward and thrust the papers hurriedly into the drawer. After which he began to bluster, as is the manner of cowards. "Pooty thing, city gals comin' hectorin' round with their airs an'—"

"Shut the drawer!" said Hildegarde, quietly.

But Simon's sluggish blood was warmed by his little bluster, and he took courage as he reflected that this was only a slight girl, and that no one else was in the house except "Old Marm," and that many broad meadows intervened between him and the farmer's stout arm. He would frighten her a bit, and get the money after all.

"We'll see about that!" he said, taking a step towards Hilda, with an evil look in his red eyes. "I'll settle a little account with you fust, my fine lady. I'll teach you to come spyin' round on me this way. Ye ain't give me a civil word sence ye come here, an' I'll pay ye—"

61

Here Simon stopped suddenly; for without a word Hildegarde had raised the pistol (which he had not seen before, as her hand was behind her), and levelled it full at his head, keeping her eyes steadily fixed on him. With a howl of terror the wretch staggered back, putting up his hands to ward off the expected shot.

"Don't shoot!" he gasped, while his color changed to a livid green. "I—I didn't mean nothin', I swar I didn't, Miss Graham. I was only—foolin'!" and he tried to smile a sickly smile; but his eyes fell before the stern glance of the gray eyes fixed so unwaveringly on him.

"Go to your room!" said Hilda, briefly. He hesitated. The lock clicked, and the girl took deliberate aim.

"I'm goin'!" shrieked the rascal, and began backing towards the door, while Hilda followed step by step, still covering him with her deadly(!) weapon. They crossed the kitchen and the back hall in this way, and Simon stumbled against the narrow stairs which led to his garret room.

"I dassn't turn round to g' up!" he whined; "ye'll shoot me in the back." No answer; but the lock clicked again, more ominously than before. He turned and fled up the stairs, muttering curses under his breath. Hildegarde closed the door at the foot of the stairs, which generally stood open, bolted it, and pushed a heavy table against it. Then she went back into the kitchen, sat down in her own little chair, and—laughed!

Yes, laughed! The absurdity of the whole episode, the ruffian quaking and fleeing before the empty pistol, her own martial fierceness and sanguinary determination, struck her with irresistible force, and peal after peal of silvery laughter rang through the kitchen. Perhaps it was partly hysterical, for her nerves were unconsciously strung to a high pitch; but she was still laughing, and still holding the terrible pistol in her hand, when Dame Hartley entered the kitchen, looking startled and uneasy.

"Dear Hilda," said the good woman, "what has been going on? I thought surely I heard a man's voice here. And—why! good gracious, child! what are you doing with that pistol?"

Hildegarde saw that there was nothing for it but to tell the simple truth, which she did in as few words as possible, trying to make light of the whole episode. But Dame Hartley was not to be deceived, and saw at once the full significance of what had happened. She was deeply moved. "My dear, brave child," she said, kissing Hilda warmly, "to think of your facing that great villain and driving him away! The courage of you! Though to be sure, any one could see it in your eyes, and your father a soldier so many of his days too."

"Oh! it was not I who frightened him," said honest Hilda, "it was the old pistol." But Nurse Lucy only shook her head and kissed her again. The thought of Simon's ingratitude and treachery next absorbed her mind, and tears of anger stood in her kind blue eyes.

"It was a black day for my poor man," she said, "when he brought that fellow to the house. I mistrusted him from the first look at his sulky face. A man who can't look you in the eyes,—well, there! that's my opinion of him!"

"Why did the farmer bring him here?" asked Hilda. "I have often wondered."

"Why, 'tis a long story, my dear," said Nurse Lucy, smoothing her apron and preparing for a comfortable chat ("For," she said, "Simon will not dare to stir from his room, even if he could get out, which he can't."). "Of all his brothers, my husband loved his brother Simon best. He was a handsome, clever fellow, Simon was. Don't you remember, my dear, Farmer speaking of him one day when you first came here, and telling how he wanted to be a gentleman; and I turned the talk when you asked what became of him?" Hilda nodded assent "Well," Nurse Lucy continued, "that was because no good came of him, and I knew it vexed Farmer to think on it, let alone Simon's son being there. It was all through his wanting to be a gentleman that Simon got into bad ways. Making friends with people who had money, he got to thinking he must have it, or must make believe he had it; so he spent all he had, and then—oh, dear!—he forged his father's name, and the farm had to be mortgaged to get him out of prison; and then he took to drinking, and went from bad to worse, and finally died in misery and wretchedness. Dear, dear! it almost broke Jacob's heart, that it did. He had tried, if ever man tried, to save his brother; but 'twas of no use. It seemed as if he was bound to ruin himself, and nothing could stop him. When he died, his wife (he married her, thinking she had money, and it turned out she hadn't a penny) took the child and went back to her own people, and we heard nothing more till about two years ago, when this boy came to Jacob with a letter from his mother's folks. She was dead, and they said they couldn't do for him any longer, and he didn't seem inclined to do for himself. Well, that is the story, Hilda dear. He has been here ever since, and he has been no comfort, no pleasure to us, I must say; but we have tried to do our duty by him, and I hoped he might feel in his heart some gratitude to his uncle, though he showed none in his actions. And now to think of it! to think of it! How shall I tell my poor man?"

"What was his mother like?" asked Hildegarde, trying to turn for the moment the current of painful thought.

Nurse Lucy gave a little laugh, even while wiping the tears from her eyes. "Poor Eliza!" she said. "She was a good woman, but—well, there! she had no faculty, as you may say. And homely! you never saw such a homely woman, Hilda; for I don't believe there could be two in the world. I never think of Eliza without remembering what Jacob said after he saw her for the first time. He'd been over to see Simon; and when he came back he walked into the kitchen and sat down, never saying a word, but just shaking his head over and over again. 'What's the matter, Jacob?' I said. 'Matter?' said he. 'Matter enough, Marm Lucy' (he's always called me Marm Lucy, my dear, since the very day we were married, though I wasn't very much older than you then). 'Simon's married,' he said, 'and I've seen his wife.' Of course I was surprised, and I wanted to know all about it. 'What sort of a girl is she?' I asked. 'Is she pretty? What color is her hair?' But Jacob put up his hand and stopped me. 'Thar!' he says, 'don't ask no questions, and I'll tell ye. Fust place, she ain't no gal, no more'n yer Aunt Saleny is!' (that was a maiden aunt of mine, dear, and well over forty at that time.) 'And what does she look like?' 'Wal! D'ye ever see an old cedar fence-rail,—one that had been chumped out with a blunt axe, and had laid out in the sun and the wind and the snow and the rain till 'twas warped this way, and shrunk that way, and twisted every way? Wal! Simon's wife looks as if she had swallowed one o' them fence-rails, and shrunk to it! Dear, dear! how I laughed. And 'twas true, my dear! It was just the way she did look. Poor soul! she led a sad life; for when Simon found he'd made a mistake about the money, there was no word too bad for him to fling at her."

At this moment Farmer Hartley's step was heard in the porch, and Nurse Lucy rose hurriedly. "Don't say anything to him, Hilda dear," she whispered,—"anything about Simon, I mean. I'll tell him to-morrow; but I don't want to trouble him to-night. This is our Faith's birthday,—seventeen year old she'd have been to-day; and it's been a right hard day for Jacob! I'll tell him about it in the morning."

Alas! when morning came it was too late. The kitchen door was swinging idly open; the desk was broken open and rifled; and Simon Hartley was gone, and with him the savings of ten years' patient labor.

CHAPTER XII.

THE OLD MILL.

It was a sad group that sat in the pleasant kitchen that bright September morning. The good farmer sat before his empty desk, seeming half stupefied by the blow which had fallen so suddenly upon him, while his wife hung about him, reproaching herself bitterly for not having put him on his guard the night before. Hildegarde moved restlessly about the kitchen, setting things to rights, as she thought, though in reality she hardly knew what she was doing, and had already carefully deposited the teapot in the coal-hod, and laid the broom on the top shelf of the dresser. Her heart was full of wrath and sorrow,—fierce anger against the miserable wretch who had robbed his benefactor; sympathy for her kind friends, brought thus suddenly from comfort to distress. For she knew now that the money which Simon had stolen had been drawn from the bank only two days before to pay off the mortgage on the farm.

"I shouldn't ha' minded the money," Farmer Hartley was saying, even now, "if I'd ha' been savin' it jest to spend or lay by. I shouldn't ha' minded, though 'twould ha' hurt jest the same to hev Simon's son take it,—my brother Simon's son, as I allus stood by. But it's hard to let the farm go. I tell ye, Marm Lucy, it's terrible hard!" and he bowed his head upon his hands in a dejection which made his wife weep anew and wring her hands.

"But they will not take the farm from you, Farmer Hartley!" cried Hilda, aghast. "They cannot do that, can they? Why, it was your father's, and your grandfather's before him."

"And his father's afore him!" said the farmer, looking up with a sad smile on his kindly face. "But that don't make no difference, ye see, Hildy. Lawyer Clinch is a hard man, a terrible hard man; and he's always wanted this farm. It's the best piece o' land in the hull township, an' he wants it for a market farm."

"But why did you mortgage it to him?" cried Hilda.

"I didn't, my gal; I didn't!" said the farmer, sadly. "He'd kep' watch over it ever sence Simon began to get into trouble,—reckon he knew pooty well how things would come out; an' bimeby Jason Doble, as held the mortgage, he up an' died, an' then Lawyer Clinch stepped in an' told the 'xecutors how Jason owed him a big debt, but he didn't want to do nothin' onfriendly, so he'd take the mortgage on Hartley's Glen and call it square. Th' executors was kind o' fool people, both on 'em—I d'no' what possessed Jason Doble to choose them for 'xecutors, when he might ha' hed the pick o' the State lunatic asylum an' got some fools as knew something; but so 'twas, an' I s'pose so 'twas meant to be. They giv' it to him, an' thanked him for takin' it; and he's waited an' waited, hopin' to ketch me in a tight place,—an' now he's done it. An' that's about all there is to it!" added Farmer Hartley, rising and pushing back his massive gray hair. "An' I sha'n't mend it by sittin' an' mowlin' over it. Thar's all Simon's work to be done, an' my own too. Huldy, my gal!" he held out his honest brown hand to Hildegarde, who clasped it affectionately in both of hers, "ye'll stay by Marm Lucy and chirk her up a bit. 'T'll be a hard day for her, an' she hasn't no gal of her own now to do for her. But ye've grown to be almost a daughter to us, Huldy. God bless ye, child!"

His voice faltered as he laid his other hand for a moment on the girl's fair head; then, turning hastily away, he took up his battered straw hat and went slowly out of the house, an older man, it might have been by ten years, than he had been the night before.

Right daughterly did Hilda show herself that day, and Faith herself could hardly have been more tender and helpful. Feeling intuitively that work was the best balm for a sore heart, she begged for Nurse Lucy's help and advice in one and another item of household routine. Then she bethought her of the churning, and felt that if this thing was to befall, it could not have better befallen than on a Tuesday, when the great blue churn stood ready in the dairy, and the cream lay thick and yellow in the shining pans.

"Well, that's a fact!" sighed Nurse Lucy. "If I hadn't forgotten my butter in all this trouble! And it must be made, sorrow or smiles, as the old saying is. Come with me, Hilda dear, if you will. Your face is the only bright thing I can see this sad day."

"EACH TOOK A SKIMMER AND SET EARNESTLY TO WORK."
"EACH TOOK A SKIMMER AND SET EARNESTLY TO WORK."
So they went together into the cool dairy, where the light came in dimly through the screen of clematis that covered the window; Hilda bared her round white arms, and Nurse Lucy pinned back her calico sleeves from a pair that were still shapely, though brown, and each took a skimmer and set earnestly to work. The process of skimming cream is in itself a soothing, not to say an absorbing one. To push the thick, yellow ripples, piling themselves upon the skimmer, across the pan; to see it drop, like melted ivory, into the cream-bowl; to pursue floating cream islands round and round the pale and mimic sea,— who can do this long, and not be comforted in some small degree, even in the midst of heavy sorrow? Also there is joy and a never-failing sense of achievement when the butter first splashes in the churn. So Nurse Lucy took heart, and churned and pressed and moulded her butter; and though some tears fell into it, it was none the worse for that.

But as she stamped each ball with the familiar stamp, showing an impossible cow with four lame legs—"How many more times," said the good woman, "shall I use this stamp; and what kind of butter will they make who come after me?" and her tears flowed again. "Lawyer Clinch keeps a hired girl, and I never saw real good butter made by a hired girl. They haven't the feeling for it; and there's feeling in butter-making as much as in anything else."

But here Hilda interposed, and gently hinted that there ought now to be "feeling" about getting the farmer's dinner. "We must have the things he likes best," she said; "for it will be hard enough to make him eat anything. I will make that apple-pudding that he likes so much; and there is the fowl for the pie, you know, Nurse Lucy."

The little maid was away on a vacation, so there was plenty of work to be done. Dinner-time came and went; and it was not till she had seen Dame Hartley safe established on her bed (for tears and trouble had brought on a sick headache), and tucked her up under the red quilt, with a bottle of hot water at her and a bowl of cracked ice by her side,—it was not till she had done this, and sung one or two of the soothing songs that the good woman loved, that Hilda had a moment to herself. She ran out to say a parting word to the farmer, who was just starting for the village in the forlorn hope, which in his heart he knew to be vain, of getting an extension of time from Lawyer Clinch while search was being made for the wretched Simon.

When old Nancy had trotted away down the lane, Hilda went back and sat down in the porch, very tired and sad at heart. It seemed so hard, so hard that she could do nothing to save her friends from the threatening ruin. She thought of her father, with a momentary flash of hope that made her spring from her seat with a half articulate cry of joy; but the hope faded as she remembered that he had probably just started for the Yosemite Valley, and that there was no knowing when or where a despatch would reach him. She sighed, and sank back on the bench with a hopeless feeling. Presently she bethought her of her little dog, whom she had not seen all day. Jock had grown very dear to her heart, and was usually her inseparable companion, except when she was busy with household tasks, to which he had an extreme aversion. A mistress, in Jock's opinion, was a person who fed one, and took one to walk, and patted one, and who was in return to be loved desperately, and obeyed in reason. But sweeping, and knocking brooms against one's legs, and paying no attention to one's invitations to play or go for a walk, were manifest derelictions from a mistress's duty; accordingly, when Hilda was occupied in the house, Jock always sat in the back porch, with his back turned to the kitchen door, and his tail cocked very high, while one ear listened eagerly for the sound of Hilda's footsteps, and the other was thrown negligently forward, to convey the impression that he did not really care, but only waited to oblige her. And the moment the door opened, and she appeared with her hat on, oh, the rapture! the shrieks and squeaks and leaps of joy, the wrigglings of body and frantic waggings of tail that ensued!

So this morning, what with all the trouble, and with her knowledge of his views, Hildegarde had not thought to wonder where Jock was. But now it struck her that she had exchanged no greeting with him since last night; that she had heard no little impatient barks, no flapping of tail against the door by way of reminder. Where could the little fellow be? She walked round the house, calling and whistling softly. She visited the barn and the cow-shed and all the haunts where her favorite was wont to linger; but no Jock was to be seen. "Perhaps he has gone over to see Will," she thought, with a feeling of relief. Indeed, this was very possible, as the two dogs were very brotherly, and frequently exchanged visits, sometimes acting as letter-carriers for their two mistresses, Pink and

Hilda. If Jock was at Pink's house, he would be well cared for, and Bubble would—but here Hildegarde started, as a new perplexity arose. Where was Bubble? They had actually forgotten the boy in the confusion and trouble of the day. He had not certainly come to the house, as he invariably did; and the farmer had not spoken of him when he came in at noon. Perhaps Pink was ill, Hilda thought, with fresh alarm. If it should be so, Bubble could not leave her, for Mrs. Chirk was nursing a sick woman two or three miles away, and there were no other neighbors nearer than the farm. "Oh, my Pink!" cried Hilda; "and I cannot go to you at once, for Nurse Lucy must not be left alone in her trouble. I must wait, wait patiently till Farmer Hartley comes back."

Patiently she tried to wait. She stole up to her room, and taking up one of her best-beloved books, "The Household of Sir Thomas More," lost herself for a while in the noble sorrows of Margaret Roper. But even this could not hold her long in her restless frame of mind, so she went downstairs again, and out into the soft, golden September air, and fell to pacing up and down the gravel walk before the house like a slender, white-robed sentinel. Presently there was a rustling in the bushes, then a hasty, joyful bark, and a little dog sprang forward and greeted Hildegarde with every demonstration of affection. "Jock! my own dear little Jock!" she cried, stooping down to caress her favorite. But as she did so she saw that it was not Jock, but Will, Pink's dog, which was bounding and leaping about her. Much puzzled, she nevertheless patted the little fellow and shook paws with him, and told him she was glad to see him. "But where is your brother?" she cried. "Oh! Willy dog, where is Jock, and where is Bubble? Bubble, Will! speak!" Will "spoke" as well as he could, giving a short bark at each repetition of the well-known name. Then he jumped up on Hilda, and threw back his head with a peculiar action which at once attracted her attention. She took him up in her arms, and lo! there was a piece of paper, folded and pinned securely to his collar. Hastily setting the dog down, she opened the note and read as follows:—

Miss Hildy,
Simon Hartley he come here early this mornin and he says to me I was diggin potaters for dinner and he come and leaned on the fence and says he I've fixed your city gal up fine he says and I says what yer mean I mean what I says he says I've fixed her up fine. She thinks a heap of that dorg I know that ain't spelled right but it's the way he said it don't she says he I reckon says I Well says he you tell her to look for him in the pit of the old mill says he. And then he larf LAUGHED I was bound I'd get it Miss Hildy I don't see why they spell a thing g and say it f and went away. And I run after him to make him tell me what he d been up to and climbin over the wall I ketched my foot on a stone and the stone come down on my foot and me with it and I didn't know anything till Simon had gone and my foot swoll up so s I couldn't walk and I wouldnt a minded its hurtin Miss Hildy but it s like there wornt no bones in it Pink says I sprante it bad and I started to go over to the Farm on all fours to tell ye but I didn't know anythin g agin and Pink made me come back. We couldnt nether on us get hold of Will but now we got him I hope he l go straite, Miss Hildy Pink wanted to write this for me but I druther write myself you aint punk tuated it she says. She can punk tuate it herself better n I can I an ti cip ate I says. From

Zerubbabel Chirk
P.S. I wisht I could get him out for ye Miss Hildy.

67

If Bubble's letter was funny, Hilda had no heart to see the fun. Her tears flowed fast as she realized the fate of her pretty little pet and playfellow. The vindictive wretch, too cowardly to face her again, had taken his revenge upon the harmless little dog. All day long poor Jock had been in that fearful place! He was still only a puppy, and she knew he could not possibly get out if he had really been thrown into the pit of the great wheel. But—and she gave a cry of pain as the thought struck her—perhaps it was only his lifeless body that was lying there. Perhaps the ruffian had killed him, and thrown him down there afterwards. She started up and paced the walk hurriedly, trying to think what she had best do. Her first impulse was to fly at once to the glen; but that was impossible, as she must not, she felt, leave Dame Hartley. No one was near: they were quite alone. Again she said, "I must wait; I must wait till Farmer Hartley comes home." But the waiting was harder now than it had been before. She could do nothing but pace up and down, up and down, like a caged panther, stopping every few minutes to throw back her head and listen for the longed-for sound,—the sound of approaching wheels.

Softly the shadows fell as the sun went down. The purple twilight deepened, and the stars lighted their silver lamps, while all the soft night noises began to make themselves heard as the voices of day died away. But Hilda had ears for only one sound. At length, out of the silence (or was it out of her own fancy?) she seemed to hear a faint, clicking noise. She listened intently: yes, there it was again. There was no mistaking the click of old Nancy's hoofs, and with it was a dim suggestion of a rattle, a jingle. Yes, beyond a doubt, the farmer was coming. Hildegarde flew into the house, and met Dame Hartley just coming down the stairs. "The farmer is coming," she said, hastily; "he is almost here. I am going to find Jock. I shall be back—" and she was gone before the astonished Dame could ask her a question.

Through the kitchen and out of the back porch sped the girl, only stopping to catch up a small lantern which hung on a nail, and to put some matches in her pocket. Little Will followed her, barking hopefully, and together the two ran swiftly through the barn-yard and past the cow-shed, and took the path which led to the old mill. The way was so familiar now to Hilda that she could have traversed it blindfold; and this was well for her, for in the dense shade of the beech-plantation it was now pitch dark. The feathery branches brushed her face and caught the tendrils of her hair with their slender fingers. There was something ghostly in their touch. Hilda was not generally timid, but her nerves had been strung to a high pitch all day, and she had no longer full control of them. She shivered, and bending her head low, called to the dog and hurried on.

Out from among the trees now, into the dim starlit glade; down the pine-strewn path, with the noise of falling water from out the beechwood at the right, and the ruined mill looming black before her. Now came the three broken steps. Yes, so far she had no need of the lantern. Round the corner, stepping carefully over the half-buried mill-stone. Groping her way, her hand touched the stone wall; but she drew it back hastily, so damp and cold the stones were. Darker and darker here; she must light the lantern before she ventured down the long flight of steps. The match spurted, and now the tiny yellow flame sprang up and shed a faint light on the immediate space around her. It only made the outer darkness seem more intense. But no matter, she could see two steps in front of her; and holding the lantern steadily before her, she stepped carefully down and down, until she stood on the firm greensward of the glen. Ah! how different everything was now from its usual aspect. The green and gold were turned into black upon black. The laughing, dimpling, sun-kissed water was now a black, gloomy pool, beyond which the fall shimmered white like a water-spirit (Undine,—or was it Kühleborn, the malignant and vengeful sprite?). The firs stood tall and gaunt, closing like a spectral guard about the ruined mill, and pointing their long, dark fingers in silent menace at the intruder upon their evening repose. Hildegarde shivered again, and held her lantern tighter, remembering how Bubble had said that the glen was "a tormentin' spooky place after dark." She looked fearfully about her as a low wind rustled the branches. They bent towards her as if to clutch her; an angry whisper seemed to pass from one to the other; and an utterly unreasoning terror fell upon the girl. She stood for a moment as if paralyzed with fear, when suddenly the little dog gave a sharp yelp, and leaped up on her impatiently. The sound startled her into new terror; but in a moment the revulsion came, and she almost laughed aloud. Here was she, a great girl, almost a woman, cowering and shivering, while a tiny puppy, who had hardly any brains at all, was eager to go on. She patted the dog, and "taking herself by both ears," as she expressed it afterwards, walked steadily forward, pushed aside the dense tangle of vines and bushes, and stooped down to enter the black hole which led into the vault of the mill.

A rush of cold air met her, and beat against her face like a black wing that brushed it. It had a mouldy smell. Holding up the lantern, Hildegarde crept as best she could through the narrow opening. A gruesome place it was in which she found herself. Grim enough by daylight, it was now doubly so; for the blackness seemed like something tangible, some shapeless monster which was gathering itself together, and shrinking back, inch by inch, as the little spark of light moved forward. The gaunt beams, the jagged bits of iron, bent and twisted into fantastic shapes, stretched and thrust themselves from every side, and again the girl fancied them fleshless arms reaching out to clutch her. But hark! was that a sound,—a faint sound from the farthest and darkest corner, where the great wheel raised its toothed and broken round from the dismal pit?

"Jock! my little Jock!" cried Hildegarde, "are you there?"

A feeble sound, the very ghost of a tiny bark, answered her, and a faint scratching was heard. In an instant all fear left Hilda, and she sprang forward, holding the lantern high above her head, and calling out words of encouragement and cheer. "Courage, Jock! Cheer up, little man! Missis is here; Missis will save you! Speak to him, Will! tell him you are here."

"Wow!" said Will, manfully, scuttling about in the darkness. "Wa-ow!" replied a pitiful squeak from the depths of the wheel-pit. Hilda reached the edge of the pit and looked down. In one corner was a little white bundle, which moved feebly, and wagged a piteous tail, and squeaked with faint rapture. Evidently the little creature was exhausted, perhaps badly injured. How should she reach him? She threw the ray of light—oh! how dim it was, and how heavy and close the darkness pressed!—on the side of the pit, and saw that it was a rough and jagged wall, with stones projecting at intervals. A moment's survey satisfied her. Setting the lantern carefully at a little distance, and bidding Will "charge" and be still, she began the descent, feeling the way carefully with her feet, and grasping the rough stones firmly with her hands. Down! down! while the huge wheel towered over her, and grinned with all its rusty teeth to see so strange a sight. At last her feet touched the soft earth; another instant, and she had Jock in her arms, and was fondling and caressing him, and saying all sorts of foolish things to him in her delight. But a cry of pain from the poor puppy, even in the midst of his frantic though feeble demonstrations of joy, told her that all was not right; and she found that one little leg hung limp, and was evidently broken. How should she ever get him up? For a moment she stood bewildered; and then an idea came to her, which she has always maintained was the only really clever one she ever had. In her pre-occupation of mind she had forgotten all day to take off the brown holland apron which she had worn at her work in the morning, and it was the touch of this apron which brought her inspiration. Quick as a flash she had it off, and tied round her neck, pinned up at both ends to form a bag. Then she stooped again to pick up Jock, whom she had laid carefully down while she arranged the apron. As she did so, the feeble ray from the lantern fell on a space where the ground had been scratched up, evidently by the puppy's paws; and in that space something shone with a dull glitter. Hildegarde bent lower, and found what seemed to be a small brass handle, half covered with earth. She dug the earth away with her hands, and pulled and tugged at the handle for some time without success; but at length the sullen soil yielded, and she staggered back against the wheel with a small metal box in her hands. No time now to examine the prize, be it what it might. Into the apron bag it went, and on top of it went the puppy, yelping dismally. Then slowly, carefully, clinging with hands and feet for life and limb, Hilda reascended the wall. Oh, but it was hard work! Her hands were already very sore, and the heavy bundle hung back from her neck and half choked her. Moreover the puppy was uncomfortable, and yelped piteously, and struggled in his bonds, while the sharp corner of the iron box pressed painfully against the back of her neck. The jutting stones were far apart, and several times it seemed as if she could not possibly reach the next one. But the royal blood was fully up. Queen Hildegarde set her teeth, and grasped the stones as if her slender hands were nerved with steel. At last! at last she felt the edge; and the next moment had dragged herself painfully over it, and stood once more on solid ground. She drew a long breath, and hastily untying the apron from her neck, took poor Jock tenderly in one arm, while with the other she carried the lantern and the iron box. Will was jumping frantically about, and trying to reach his brother puppy, who responded with squeaks of joy to his enraptured greeting.

"Down, Will!" said Hilda, decidedly. "Down, sir! Lie still, Jocky! we shall be at home soon now. Patience, little dog!" And Jock tried hard to be patient; though it was not pleasant to be squeezed into a ball while his mistress crawled out of the hole, which she did with some difficulty, laden with her triple burden.

However, they were out at last, and speeding back towards the farm as fast as eager feet could carry them. Little thought had Hilda now of spectral trees or ghostly gloom. Joyfully she hurried back, up the long steps, along the glade, through the beach-plantation; only laughing now when the feathery fingers brushed her face, and hugging Jock so tight that he squeaked again. Now she saw the lights twinkling in the farm-house, and quickening her pace, she fairly ran through lane and barnyard, and finally burst into the kitchen, breathless and exhausted, but radiant. The farmer and his wife, who were sitting with disturbed and anxious looks, rose hastily as she entered.

"Oh, Hilda, dear!" cried Dame Hartley, "we have been terribly frightened about you. Jacob has been searching—But, good gracious, child!" she added, breaking off hastily, "where have you been, and what have you been doing to get yourself into such a state!"

70

Well might the good woman exclaim, while the farmer gazed in silent astonishment. The girl's dress was torn and draggled, and covered with great spots and splashes of black. Her face was streaked with dirt, her fair hair hanging loose upon her shoulders. Could this be Hilda, the dainty, the spotless? But her eyes shone like stars, and her face, though very pale, wore a look of triumphant delight.

"I have found him!" she said, simply. "My little Jock! Simon threw him into the wheel-pit of the old mill, and I went to get him out. His leg is broken, but I know you can set it, Nurse Lucy. Don't look so frightened," she added, smiling, seeing that the farmer and his wife were fairly pale with horror; "it was not so very bad, after all." And in as few words as might be, she told the story of Bubble's note and of her strange expedition.

"My child! my child!" cried Dame Hartley, putting her arms round the girl, and weeping as she did so. "How could you do such a fearful thing? Think, if your foot had slipped you might be lying there now yourself, in that dreadful place!" and she shuddered, putting back the tangle of fair hair with trembling fingers.

"Ah, but you see, my foot didn't slip, Nurse Lucy!" replied Hilda, gayly. "I wouldn't let it slip! And here I am safe and sound, so it's really absurd for you to be frightened now, my dear!"

"Why in the name of the airthly didn't ye wait till I kem home, and let me go down for ye?" demanded the farmer, who was secretly delighted with the exploit, though he tried to look very grave.

"Oh! I—I never thought of it!" said Hildegarde. "My only thought was to get down there as quickly as possible. So I waited till I heard you coming, for I didn't want to leave Nurse Lucy alone; and then—I went! And I will not be scolded," she added quickly, "for I think I have made a great discovery." She held one hand behind her as she spoke, and her eyes sparkled as she fixed them on the farmer. "Dear Farmer Hartley," she said, "is it true, as Bubble told me, that your father used to go down often into the vault of the old mill?"

"Why, yes, he did, frequent!" said the farmer, wondering. "'Twas a fancy of his, pokin' about thar. But what—"

"Wait a moment!" cried Hilda, trembling with excitement. "Wait a moment! Think a little, dear Farmer Hartley! Did you not tell me that when he was dying, your father said something about digging? Try to remember just what he said!"

The farmer ran his hand through his shaggy locks with a bewildered look. "What on airth are ye drivin' at, Hildy?" he said. "Father? why, he didn't say nothin' at the last, 'cept about them crazy di'monds he was allus jawin' about. 'Di'monds' says he. And then he says 'Dig!' an' fell back on the piller, an' that was all."

"Yes!" cried Hilda. "And you never did dig, did you? But now somebody has been digging. Little Jock began, and I finished; and we have found—we have found—" She broke off suddenly, and drawing her hand from behind her back, held up the iron box. "Take it!" she cried, thrusting it into the astonished farmer's hands, and falling on her

71

knees beside his chair. "Take it and open it! I think—oh! I am sure—that you will not lose the farm after all. Open it quickly, please!"

Now much agitated in spite of himself, Farmer Hartley bent himself to the task of opening the box. For some minutes it resisted stubbornly, and even when the lock was broken, the lid clung firmly, and the rusted hinges refused to perform their office. But at length they yielded, and slowly, unwillingly, the box opened. Hilda's breath came short and quick, and she clasped her hands unconsciously as she bent forward to look into the mysterious casket. What did she see?

"'TAKE IT AND OPEN IT!'"
"'TAKE IT AND OPEN IT!'"
At first nothing but a handkerchief,—a yellow silk handkerchief, of curious pattern, carefully folded into a small square and fitting nicely inside the box. That was all; but Farmer Hartley's voice trembled as he said, in a husky whisper, "Father's hankcher!" and it was with a shaking hand that he lifted the folds of silk. One look—and he fell back in his chair, while Hildegarde quietly sat down on the floor and cried. For the diamonds were there! Big diamonds and little diamonds,—some rough and dull, others flashing out sparks of light, as if they shone the brighter for their long imprisonment; some tinged with yellow or blue, some with the clear white radiance which is seen in nothing else save a dewdrop when the morning sun first strikes upon it. There they lay,—a handful of stones, a little heap of shining crystals; but enough to pay off the mortgage on Hartley's Glen and leave the farmer a rich man for life.

Dame Hartley was the first to rouse herself from the silent amaze into which they had fallen. "Well, well!" she said, wiping her eyes, "the ways of Providence are mysterious. To think of it, after all these years! Why, Jacob! Come, my dear, come! You ain't crying, now that the Lord, and this blessed child under Him, has taken away all your trouble?"

But the farmer, to his own great amazement, was crying. He sobbed quietly once or twice, then cleared his throat, and wiped his eyes with the old silk handkerchief. "Poor ol' father," he said, simply. "It seems kind o' hard that nobody ever believed him, an' we let him die thinkin' he was crazy. That takes holt on me; it does, Marm Lucy, now I tell ye! Seems like's if I'd been punished for not havin' faith, and now I git the reward without havin' deserved it."

"As if you could have reward enough!" cried Hildegarde, laying her hand on his affectionately. "But, oh! do just look at them, dear Farmer Hartley! Aren't they beautiful? But what is that peeping out of the cotton-wool beneath? It is something red."

Farmer Hartley felt beneath the cotton which lined the box, and drew out—oh, wonderful! a chain of rubies! Each stone glowed like a living coal as he held it up in the lamp-light. Were they rubies, or were they drops of blood linked together by a thread of gold?

"The princess's necklace!" cried Hilda. "Oh, beautiful! beautiful! And I knew it was true! I knew it all the time."

72

The old man fixed a strange look, solemn and tender, on the girl as she stood at his side, radiant and glowing with happiness. "She said—" his voice trembled as he spoke, "that furrin woman—she said it was her heart's blood as father had saved. And now it's still blood, Hildy, my gal, our heart's blood, that goes out to you, and loves and blesses you as if you were our own child come back from the dead." And drawing her to him, he clasped the ruby chain round Hilda's neck.

CHAPTER XIII.

THE TREE-PARTY.

Another golden day! But the days would all be golden now, thought Hildegarde. "Oh, how different it is from yesterday!" she cried to Nurse Lucy as she danced about the kitchen. "The sun shone yesterday, but it did us no good. To-day it warms my heart, the good sunshine. And yesterday the trees seemed to mock me, with all their scarlet and gold; but to-day they are dressed up to celebrate our good fortune. Let us call them in to rejoice with us, Nurse Lucy. Let us have a tree-party, instead of a tea-party!"

"My dear," said Dame Hartley, looking up with a puzzled smile, "what do you mean?"

"Oh! I don't mean to invite the whole forest to supper," said Hildegarde, laughing. "But you shall see, Nurse Lucy; you shall see. Just wait till this afternoon. I must run now over to Pink's, and tell her all the wonderful things that have happened, and see how poor Bubble is."

Away she went like a flash, through the golden fields, down the lane, where the maples made a flaming tent of scarlet over her head, bursting suddenly like a whirlwind into the little cottage, where the brother and sister, both now nearly helpless, sat waiting with pale and anxious faces. At sight of her Pink uttered a cry of delight, while Bubble flushed with pleasure; and both were about to pour out a flood of eager questions, when Hilda laid her hand over Pink's mouth and made a sign to the boy. "Two minutes to get my breath!" she cried, panting; "only two, and then you shall hear all." She spent the two minutes in filling the kettle and presenting Bubble with a pot of peach-marmalade that Dame Hartley had sent him; then, sitting down by the invalid's chair, she told from beginning to end the history of the past two days. The recital was thrilling enough, and before it was over the pale cheeks were crimson, and the two pairs of blue eyes blazed with excitement.

"Oh!" cried Bubble, hopping up and down in his chair, regardless of the sprained ankle. "Oh, I say, Miss Hildy! I dunno what to say! Wouldn't he ha' liked it, though? My! 'twas jest like himself. Jes' exactly what he'd ha' done."

"What who would have done, Bubble?" asked Hilda, laughing.

"Why, him! Buckle-oh!" said the boy. "I was jest sayin' over the ballid when I saw ye comin'. Warn't it like him, Pink, say?"

But Pink drew the stately head down towards her, and kissed the glowing cheek, and whispered, "Queen Hildegarde! my queen!"

The tears started to Hilda's eyes as she returned the kiss; but she brushed them away, and rose hastily, announcing her intention of "setting things to rights" against Mrs. Chirk's return. "You poor dears!" she cried, "how did you manage yesterday? If I had only known, I would have come and got dinner for you."

"Oh! we got on very well indeed," replied Pink, laughing, "though there were one or two mishaps. Fortunately there was plenty of bread in the cupboard, where we could easily reach it; and with that and the molasses jug, we were in no danger of starvation. But Mother had left a custard-pie on the upper shelf, and poor Bubble wanted a piece of it for dinner. But neither of us cripples could get at it; and for a long time we could think of no plan which would make it possible. At last Bubble had a bright idea. You remember the big fork that Mother uses to take pies out of the oven? Well, he spliced that on to the broom-handle, and then, standing well back, so that he could see (on one foot, of course, for he couldn't put the other to the ground), he reached for the pie. It was a dreadful moment, Hilda! The pie slid easily on to the fork, and for a moment all seemed to promise well; but the next minute, just as Bubble began to lower it, he wavered on his one foot—only a little, but enough to send the poor pie tumbling to the ground."

"Poor pie!" cried Bubble. "Wal, I like that! Poor me, I sh'd say. I'd had bread'n m'lasses three meals runnin', Miss Hildy. Now don't you think that old pie might ha' come down straight?"

"You should have seen his face, poor dear!" cried Pink. "He really couldn't laugh— for almost two minutes."

"Wal, I s'pose 'twas kind o' funny," the boy admitted, while Hilda laughed merrily over the catastrophe. "But thar! when one's used to standin' on two legs, it's dretful onhandy tryin' to stand on one. We'll have bread and jam to-day," he added, with an affectionate glance at the pot of marmalade, "and that's a good enough dinner for the Governor o' the State."

"Indeed, you shall have more than that!" cried Hildegarde. "Nurse Lucy does not need me before dinner, so I will get your dinner for you."

So the active girl made up the fire anew, swept the floor, dusted tables and chairs, and made the little room look tidy and cheerful, as Pink loved to see it. Then she ran down to the cellar, and reappeared with a basket of potatoes and a pan of rosy apples.

"Now we will perform a trio!" she said. "Pink, you shall peel and core the apples for apple-sauce, and Bubble shall pare the potatoes, while I make biscuit and gingerbread."

Accordingly, she rolled up her sleeves and set busily to work; the others followed her example, and fingers and tongues moved ceaselessly, in cheerful emulation of each other.

"I'd like to git hold o' Simon Hartley!" said Bubble, slicing vengefully at a big potato. "I wish't he was this tater, so I do! I'd skin him! Yah! ornery critter! An' him standin' thar an' grinnin' at me over the wall, an' I couldn't do nothin'! Seemed's though I sh'd fly, Miss Hildy, it did; an' then not to be able to crawl even! I sw—I tell ye, now, I didn't like that."

"Poor Bubble!" said Hilda, compassionately, "I'm sure you didn't. And did he really start to crawl over to the farm, Pink?"

"Indeed he did!" replied Pink. "Nothing that I could say would keep him from trying it; so I bandaged his ankle as well as I could, and off he started. But he fainted twice before he got to the gate, so there was nothing for it but to crawl back again, and—have the knees of his trousers mended."

"Dear boy!" said Hilda, patting the curly head affectionately. "Good, faithful boy! I shall think a great deal more of it, Bubble, than if you had been able to walk all the way. And, after all," she added, "I am glad I had to do it myself,—go down to the mill, I mean. It is something to remember! I would not have missed it."

"No more wouldn't I!" cried Bubble, enthusiastically. "I'd ha' done it for ye twenty times, ye know that, Miss Hildy; but I druther ha' hed you do it;" and Hildegarde understood him perfectly.

The simple meal prepared and set out, Hilda bade farewell to her two friends, and flitted back to the farm. Mrs. Chirk was to return in the evening, so she felt no further anxiety about them.

She found the farmer just returned from the village in high spirits. Squire Gaylord had examined the diamonds, pronounced them of great value, and had readily advanced the money to pay off the mortgage, taking two or three large stones as security. Lawyer Clinch had reluctantly received his money, and relinquished all claim upon Hartley's Glen, though with a very bad grace.

"He kind o' insinuated that the di'monds had prob'ly ben stole by Father or me, he couldn't say which; and he said somethin' about inquirin' into the matter. But Squire Gaylord shut him up pooty quick, by sayin' thar was more things than that as might be inquired into, and if he began, others might go on; and Lawyer Clinch hadn't nothin' more to say after that."

When dinner was over, and everything "redded up," Hildegarde sent Dame Hartley upstairs to take a nap, and escorted the farmer as far as the barn on his way to the turnip-field. Then, "the coast being clear," she said to herself, "we will prepare for the tree-party."

Accordingly, arming herself with a stout pruning-knife, she took her way to the "wood-lot," which lay on the north side of the house. The splendor of the trees, which were now in full autumnal glory, gave Hilda a sort of rapture as she approached them. What had she ever seen so beautiful as this,—the shifting, twinkling myriads of leaves, blazing with every imaginable shade of color above the black, straight trunks; the deep, translucent blue of the sky bending above; the golden light which transfused the whole scene; the crisp freshness of the afternoon air? She wanted to sing, to dance, to do everything that was joyous and free. But now she had work to do. She visited all her favorite trees,—the purple ash, the vivid, passionate maples, the oaks in their sober richness of murrey and crimson. On each and all she levied contributions, cutting armful after armful, and carried them to the house, piling them in splendid heaps on the shed-floor. Then, after carefully laying aside a few specially perfect branches, she began the work of decoration. Over the chimney-piece she laid great boughs of maple, glittering like purest gold in the afternoon light, which streamed broadly in through the windows. Others—scarlet, pink, dappled red, and yellow—were placed over the windows, the doors, the dresser. She filled the corners with stately oak-boughs, and made a bower of the purple ash in the bow-window,—Faith's window. Then she set the tea-table with the best china, every plate and dish resting on a mat of scarlet leaves, while a chain of yellow ones outlined the shining square board. A tiny scarlet wreath encircled the tea-kettle, and even the butter-dish displayed its golden balls beneath an arch of flaming crimson. This done, she filled a great glass bowl with purple-fringed asters and long, gleaming sprays of golden-rod, and setting it in the middle of the table, stood back with her head a little on one side and surveyed the general effect.

"Good!" was her final comment; "very good! And now for my own part."

She gathered in her apron the branches first selected, and carried them up to her own room, where she proceeded to strip off the leaves and to fashion them into long garlands. As her busy fingers worked, her thoughts flew hither and thither, bringing back the memories of the past few days. Now she stood in the kitchen, pistol in hand, facing the rascal Simon Hartley; and she laughed to think how he had shaken and cowered before the empty weapon. Now she was in the vault of the ruined mill, with a thousand horrors of darkness pressing on her, and only the tiny spark of light in her lantern to keep off the black and shapeless monsters. Now she thought of the kind farmer, with a throb of pity, as she recalled the hopeless sadness of his face the night before. Just the very night before, only a few hours; and now how different everything was! Her heart gave a little happy thrill to think that she, Hilda, the "city gal," had been able to help these dear friends in their trouble. They loved her already, she knew that; they would love her more now. Ah! and they would miss her all the more, now that she must leave them so soon.

Then, like a flash, her thoughts reverted to the plan she had been revolving in her mind two days before, before all these strange things had happened. It was a delightful little plan! Pink was to be sent to a New York hospital,—the very best hospital that could be found; and Hildegarde hoped—she thought—she felt almost sure that the trouble could be greatly helped, if not cured altogether. And then, when Pink was well, or at least a great, great deal better, she was to come and live at the farm, and help Nurse Lucy, and sing to the farmer, and be all the comfort—no, not all, but nearly the comfort that Faith would have been if she had lived. And Bubble—yes! Bubble must go to school,—to a good school, where his bright, quick mind should learn everything there was to learn. Papa would see to that, Hilda knew he would. Bubble would delight Papa! And then he would go to college, and by and by become a famous doctor, or a great lawyer, or—oh! Bubble could be anything he chose, she was sure of it.

So the girl's happy thoughts flew on through the years that were to come, weaving golden fancies even as her fingers were weaving the gay chains of shining leaves; but let us hope the fancy-chains, airy as they were, were destined to become substantial realities long after the golden wreaths had faded.

But now the garlands were ready, and none too soon; for the shadows were lengthening, and she heard Nurse Lucy downstairs, and Farmer Hartley would be coming in soon to his tea. She took from a drawer her one white frock, the plain lawn which had once seemed so over-plain to her, and with the wreaths of scarlet and gold she made a very wonderful thing of it. Fifteen minutes' careful work, and Hilda stood looking at her image in the glass, well pleased and a little surprised; for she had been too busy of late to think much about her looks, and had not realized how sun and air and a free, out-door life had made her beauty blossom and glow like a rose in mid-June. With a scarlet chaplet crowning her fair locks, bands of gold about waist and neck and sleeves, and the whole skirt covered with a fantastic tracery of mingled gold and fire, she was a vision of almost startling loveliness. She gave a little happy laugh. "Dear old Farmer!" she said, "he likes to see me fine. I think this will please him." And light as a thistledown, the girl floated downstairs and danced into the kitchen just as Farmer Hartley entered it from the other side.

"Highty-tighty!" cried the good man, "what's all this? Is there a fire? Everything's all ablaze! Why, Hildy! bless my soul!" He stood in silent delight, looking at the lovely figure before him, with its face of rosy joy and its happy, laughing eyes.

"It's a tree-party," explained Hildegarde, taking his two hands and leading him forward. "I'm part of it, you see, Farmer Hartley. Do you like it? Is it pretty? It's to celebrate our good fortune," she added; and putting her arm in the old man's, she led him about the room, pointing out the various decorations, and asking his approval.

Farmer Hartley admired everything greatly, but in an absent way, as if his mind were preoccupied with other matters. He turned frequently towards the door, as if he expected some one to follow him. "All for me?" he kept asking. "All for me and Marm Lucy, Hildy? Ye—ye ain't expectin' nobody else to tea, now?"

"No," said Hilda, wondering. "Of course not. Who else is there to come? Bubble has sprained his ankle, you know, and Pink—"

"Yes, yes; I know, I know!" said the farmer, still with that backward glance at the door. And then, as he heard some noise in the yard, he added hurriedly: "At the same time, ye know, Hildy, people do sometimes drop in to tea—kind o' onexpected-like, y' understand. And—and—all this pretty show might—might seem to—indicate, ye see—"

"Jacob Hartley? what are you up to?" demanded Nurse Lucy, rather anxiously, as she stood at the shed-door watching him intently. "Does your head feel dizzy? You'd better go and lie down; you've had too much excitement for a man of—"

"Oh, you thar, Marm Lucy?" cried the farmer, with a sigh of relief that was half a chuckle, "Now, thar! you tell Hildy that folks does sometimes drop in—onexpected-like—folks from a consid'able distance sometimes. Why, I've known 'em—" But here he stopped suddenly. And as Hilda, expecting she knew not what, stood with hands clasped together, and beating heart, the door was thrown open and a strong, cheery voice cried, "Well, General!" Another moment, and she was clasped in her father's arms.

THE LAST WORD.

The lovely autumn is gone, and winter is here. Mr. and Mrs. Graham have long since been settled at home, and Hildegarde is with them. How does it fare with her, the new Hildegarde, under the old influences and amid the old surroundings? For answer, let us take the word of her oldest friend,—the friend who "knows Hildegarde!" Madge Everton has just finished a long letter to Helen McIvor, who is spending the winter in Washington, and there can be no harm in our taking a peep into it.

"You ask me about Hilda Graham; but, alas! I have nothing pleasant to tell. My dear, Hilda is simply lost to us! It is all the result of that dreadful summer spent among swineherds. You know what the Bible says! I don't know exactly what, but something terrible about that sort of thing. Of course it is partly her mother's influence as well. I have always dreaded it for Hilda, who is so sensitive to impressions. Why, I remember, as far back as the first year that we were at Mme. Haut-Ton's, Mrs. Graham saying to Mamma, 'I wish we could interest our girls a little in sensible things!' My dear, she meant hospitals and soup-kitchens and things! And Mamma said (you know Mamma isn't in the least afraid of Mrs. Graham, though I confess I am!), 'My dear Mrs. Graham, if there is one thing Society will not tolerate, it is a sensible woman. Our girls might as well have the small-pox at once, and be done with it.' Wasn't it clever of Mamma? And Mrs. Graham just looked at her as if she were a camel from Barnum's.

"Well, poor Hildegarde is sensible enough now to satisfy even her mother. Ever since she came home from that odious place, it has been one round of hospitals and tenement-houses and sloughs of horror. I don't mean that she has given up school, for she is studying harder than ever; but out of school she is simply swallowed up by these wretched things. I have remonstrated with her almost on my knees. 'Hildegarde,' I said one day, 'do you realize that you are practically giving up your whole life? If you once lose your place in Society among those of your own age and position, you NEVER can regain it. Do you realize this, Hilda? for I feel it a solemn duty to warn you!' My dear, she actually laughed! and only said, 'Dear Madge, I have only just begun to have any life!' And that was all I could get out of her, for just then some one came in. But even this is not the worst! Oh, Helen! she has some of the creatures whom she saw this summer, actually staying in the house,—in that house, which we used to call Castle Graham, and were almost afraid to enter ourselves, so stately and beautiful it was! There are two of these creatures,—a girl about our age, some sort of dreadful cripple, who goes about in a bath-chair, and a freckled imp of a boy. The girl is at ―― Hospital for treatment, but spends every Sunday at the Grahams', and Hilda devotes most of her spare time to her. The boy is at school,—one of the best schools in the city. 'But who are these people?' I hear you cry. My dear! they are simply ignorant paupers, who were Hilda's constant companions through that disastrous summer. Now their mother is dead, and the people with whom Hilda stayed have adopted them. The boy is to be a doctor, and the girl is going to get well, Dr. George says. (He calls her a beautiful and interesting creature; but you know what that means. Any diseased creature is beautiful to him!) Well, and these, my dear Helen, are Hilda Graham's friends, for whom she has deserted her old ones! for though she is unchanged towards me when I see her, I hardly ever do see her. She cares nothing

78

for my pursuits, and I certainly have no intention of joining in hers. I met her the other day on Fifth Avenue, walking beside that odious bath-chair, which the freckled boy was pushing. She looked so lovely (for she is prettier than ever, with a fine color and eyes like stars), and was talking so earnestly, and walking somehow as if she were treading on air, it sent a pang through my heart. I just paused an instant (for though I trust I am not snobbish, Helen, still, I draw the line at bath-chairs, and will not be seen standing by one), and said in a low tone, meant only for her ear, 'Ah! has Queen Hildegarde come to this?' My dear, she only laughed! But that girl, that cripple, looked up with a smile and a sort of flash over her face, and said, just as if she knew me, 'Yes, Miss Everton! the Queen has come to her kingdom!'"

THE END

Printed in the USA
CPSIA information can be obtained
at www.ICGtesting.com
LVHW011837190324
774850LV00055B/1610